"You must
ESCAPE
the
FAIRYTALE"

FIRST EDITION

ISBN 978-1-990690-56-3 (PRINT) ISBN 978-1-990690-57-0 (PDF) ISBN 978-1-990690-58-7 (EPUB)

PUBLISHED BY STRANGER FICTION INC. 716 - 70 Arthur Street, Winnipeg, Manitoba, Canada R3B 1G7

www.StrangerFiction.ca

Printed in Canada

Welcome to

the Storybook PROGRAM

Life is not a Fairy Tale, but it could be.

"We tell ourselves stories in order to live..."

— Joan Didion, The White Album

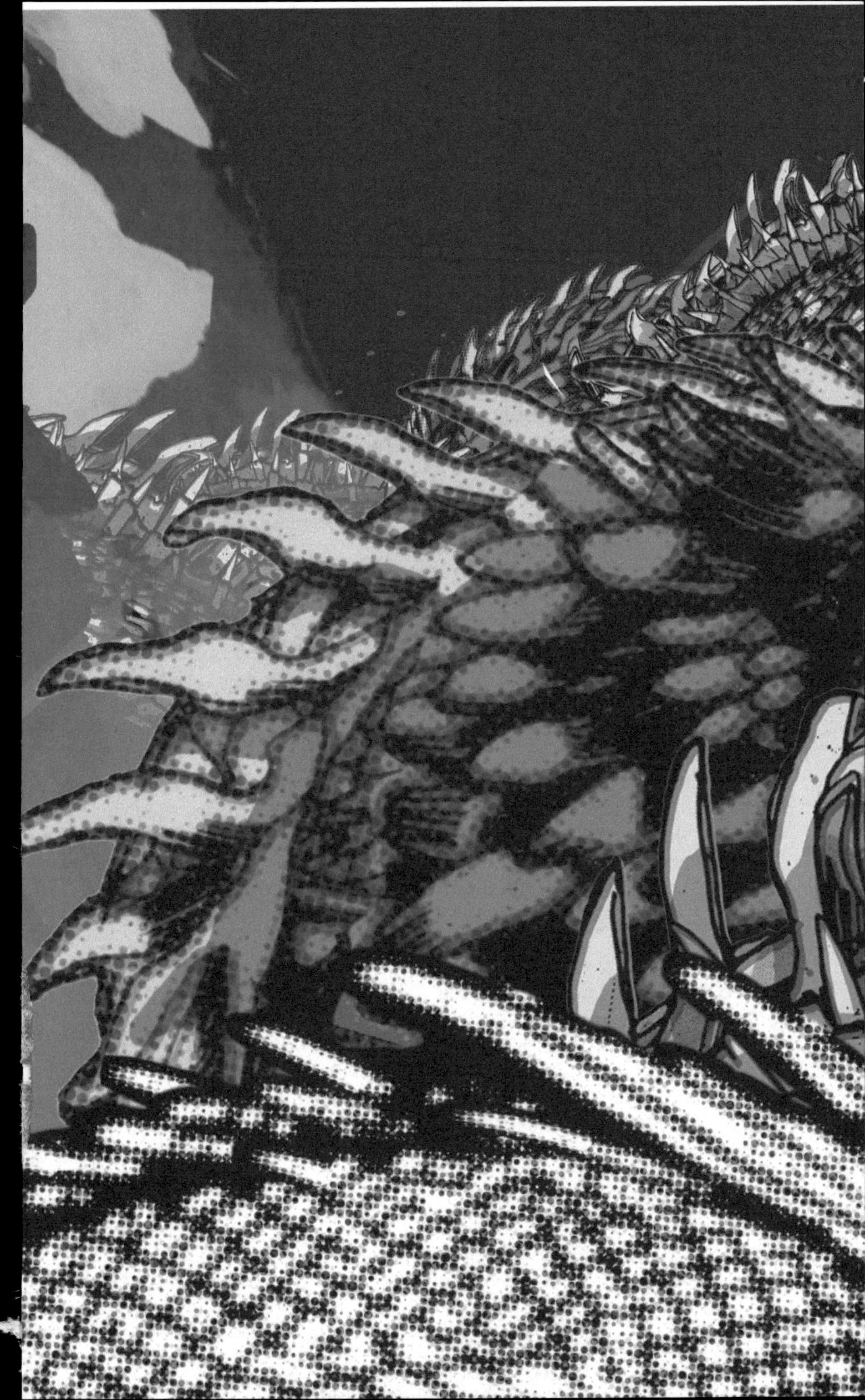

BRING A FLASHLIGHT.

When a friend says, "I want you to come see something with me, bring a flashlight," my first instinct, often contrary to self-preservation, is usually "whose car are we taking?"

The story of making a book, an illustration, a design, or a movie of any kind is never a simple story. It took years for us to arrive anywhere, but the journey sure was fun.

It all started when I went looking for a flashlight to go explore an abandoned building and basement complex with a friend during the shutdown of the film business in the middle of a global pandemic. Filmmaker and friend Micheal Sanders gave me access to a old, labyrinthine RCMP forensic lab during a location scout. The idea that we (and many others) had was that with a very small crew and a very small cast and a closed set, we could still make fun things and keep people safe.

This exploration gave us several ideas for film scripts and treatments that we wrote but never produced. The Princess and the Dragon began this way. I worked on a treatment of my own and pitched the idea as something to invest in and the answer was "no." We kept working the other ideas instead. Those stories will end well, I believe, but elsewhere.

I liked The Princess and The Dragon too much and felt I had to make it into something, somehow. It was a challenging idea for me, and that made it interesting. I was also interested in working further with collaborator and friend Dr. Jonathan Ball. So we co-wrote the story, sending drafts back and forth. We finished it and put it somewhere.

Years later, another filmmaker, Miles Crossman, who was there to see me about production design for a different film project, got a call that changed the vibe of the meeting. He was about to lose his shooting window on an abandoned sanitarium on a hill, and he needed a small-budget horror script idea in a hurry. "Oh, is that all?" I said. "That's something we do a lot around here..." and so I showed him a bunch of pitches we had worked up. The basic description and premise of The Princess and The Dragon lit a spark in him. "That one," he said.

Jonathan and I visited the location site in all its dilapidated, haunting glory and created a new scriptment based on our prose story, both of which are presented here. As we adapted the story, we realized that it fit nicely with my Minus Institute book/graphic novel/game project, which already had a large amount of finished design work we could use, so I included that too. In independent productions, every scrap can feel like a meal.

Our scriptment was significantly rewritten by Miles and Erik Fjeldsted (executive producer on the project). "It's not quite the movie I want to make," Miles said, "but it's a great start."

After being rewritten, Jonathan and I offered further revisions, but soon had to switch hats to become producers, defending the new script from those meddlesome writers. Laughing as we said, "that's got to go" to portions of our very own story we had agonized over just weeks before.

I loved Miles and Erik's idea of the Storybook Program having an actual storybook as a prop, with torn pages making a clue path in the story. So, I worked round the clock for about 10 days to make one before shooting started. Muttering rhymes to myself as if possessed as I floated around my home and family, suddenly having volunteered to make the thing real. I glued those pages into gutted and reskinned Disney storybooks and weathered them. Suddenly, we had the props, pages, and poems that then fleshed out the central concept of the finished film.

During post-production, I made a Princess and the Dragon tabletop roleplaying game that I ran at a variety of local conventions with my own Danger in the Details rules.

Clearly the warning of The Princess and The Dragon (to be careful which stories you let take over your life) was one I needed but had not heeded.

Now, this book collects a great deal of that whole creative experience and design work, and a feature-length independent movie based on and incorporating much of this material now also exists. Maybe that film brought you here, maybe this book will bring you to it. How the made-up world affects the real one is strange indeed.

So pick up a flashlight and go looking. Who knows what there is to find?

GMB Chomichuk

IT SHOULD BE HARD TO SPEAK OF TERRIBLE THINGS.

I had settled on this as the core of what I felt was wrong with the horror I had been reading.

The trend in modern horror at the time (when Gregory came to me with the idea of writing a short story based on his idea) was to use clean, transparent prose. I understood its purpose. Get the narrator out of the way, and let the events of the story be the focus.

But I had been reading Harlan Ellison and Tony Burgess and felt horror would work better if you brought a distorted perspective to the prose. If the storytelling narrator was affected by what was happening. The horror's traumatic power should transcend the story's world and start affecting our own. In Stephen King's terms, the goal should be to hurt the reader.

Lovecraft understood this, but could be wordy and awkward. Experimentalists often pushed things too far, so that the horror bled away. Was it possible to seek a middle ground? Could I present an unstable narrative voice, allow some elements of the story to become distorted and surreal, and let other elements be communicated clearly so that their frightful aspects were both understood and felt?

Gregory and I had worked on many projects over the years, including one of the film treatments set in the forensic laboratory that he talks about in his introduction. I was a bit disappointed when that one didn't move forward, because I felt it had the makings of a great film, so when he proposed taking his Princess and the Dragon idea and fleshing it out, I suggested we make it a short story instead. Then we could publish it even if the project didn't advance.

We sent the story around to literary journals, but they all rejected it, saying it was too mainstream or too experimental. That made me happy, because I had wanted to hit that middle-ground in the first place. It has also been my experience that if everyone rejects a story for different reasons, then they are all wrong and it is one of your best stories. When you finally put it in a book, readers single it out as their favourite story. I've had that kind of thing happen many times. We ultimately published the story independently as an short ebook.

When Miles and Erik asked us to adapt it and come on as co-producers of an independent feature, and we put together our scriptment for them, we had in mind 1980s horror movies like those of John Carpenter. These often lay out the basic monster and premise quickly and then move forward aggressively, no looking back.

I was also thinking of the Alien script by Walter Hill and David Giler, based on the earlier screenplay by Dan O'Bannon. I consider the Hill and Giler draft to be one of the world's great scripts, much better than the O'Bannon draft (heresy, I know). It's minimalistic, imagistic, action-packed, and sets the tone perfectly. It has the power and brevity of haiku at times.

This is why you can read our scriptment and watch the film and see how one led to the other but also see massive differences even when the film remains close to the script. This is best shown in the tone of the twist ending. Miles and Erik shifted away from feminist subversion of slasher tropes toward EC Horror-style shock by way of a '90s horror film sensibility. This makes more sense for their film, which centres on themes of oppression and madness. Our scriptment instead focuses on themes of transformation and self-possession via the shared obsession Gregory and I have with surrealism and semiotics.

Although we were sad to see certain elements go, once Miles and Erik moved away from our claustrophobic development of the concept, and opened things up, it created space for us to come back in and add even more elements from Gregory's preexisting Minus Institute project and a related Storybook Program spinoff idea. Not only did this increase the production value, it offered space for us to expand the film's world by extending ideas in the story that bled naturally into Gregory's Minus Institute work.

This book you're holding represents the culmination of all of our work prior to the film project, and some of the work during the film project that we maintained separated rights to, and is meant to stand alone as its own hybrid, transmedia, experimental story. At the same time, we hope you enjoy it as a companion piece to the film, which we're proud to have helped Miles and Erik realize according to their visions.

Dr Jonathan Ball

EPIGRAPH TEXT
"All men dream, but not
equally. Those who dream by
night in the dusty recesses of
their minds wake in the day to
find that it was vanity: but
the dreamers of the day are
dangerous men, for they act
their dream with open eyes, to
make it possible."
-- T. E. Lawrence
START

Dr. Storybook

DR STORYBOOK
Part of your problem, Jenna, is
that you're rejecting reality.

In The Castle.

The Princess.

He woke inside of an Old Story.

Hung in the air. Upside down. Blood swarmed in his head.

The churn of swaying motion when he moved. He hung by his feet. He knew he hung because of the blood in his head but The Princess knew nothing else, saw nothing through the covering tight against his face. No eye, mouth, or nose holes in its tight-stretched canvas.

The Princess knew that this was wrong, that he must have memories. Mind fogged from the blood and something else, something that killed the past and future in his thoughts and left the taste of metal in his mouth. But still, though he knew nothing, he knew this:

He was in danger.

His hands ached, swollen. He moved them to his face. Tugging off the canvas, not a covering after all but a mask, which he pulled from his face. His wrists were wrapped together by cords of rough leather. He looked up, which was down and saw and felt more tight binding. Leather cords wrapping his midsection, making it hard to breathe, hard to bend. His legs were similarly wrapped, bound feet hooked to a chain.

He held up his fingers like a screen against the world rushing into them. Then looked down and on the floor beneath him the mask, which had fallen, looked back at him. Painted white, a storybook Princess face, with black lips and lashes and a thin, painted crown.

Arclight tore at his eyes and he blinked in the brightness. A few metres from him was an idol or effigy like those built of piled stones in other places — this one was made of power tools, rusting toolboxes, paint cans, oil cans, greasy cardboard. A tangle of extension cords and a string of bare white bulbs wrapped around the pile, which was bound up by rusty barbed wire into an approximation of a human shape.

He was in the courtyard of The Castle. A romantic metaphor laid over a cruel reality. A world of concrete, steel, and harsh electric light.

He hung in a garage bay, massive, able to hold a half-dozen cars up on hoists. Rolling doors, closed, ran one whole wall into darkness. His feet were lashed by a rope to a vehicle hoist that held him aloft.

Just a few feet of air between the top of his head and a floor of plywood that covered a car-servicing pit. Overturned tool carts everywhere, empty red metal trays strewn about. The electric-light effigy stood between The Princess and a large metal door that was open. The dim illumination from the effigy's string of lights turned the hall into a yawning tunnel of cluttered shadows.

The hall that led deeper into The Castle.

"The Princess is alone in The Castle with The Dragon. This is an Old Story." The voice a memory without a source, without detail. He knew nothing, knew not who told him this, knew not if this was a warning or a promise. Still, though he remembered nothing, he recognized The Dragon when it came.

For it came.

Then, down the hall, The Dragon.

She stopped and stood with her head to the side. Face covered in her own mask — triangular, black leather with red markings, designs that swirled and tore outward as if bleeding away from the horror of her eyes. Her eyes the only thing visible through the mask, its tight fabric closing over her mouth. The Dragon looked down at the white mask on the floor then tilted her tortured face up to regard The Princess.

Had she been waiting for him to wake? She tilted her expressionless mask upward, standing at attention now. She raised her hands before her, between them. In each hand she held a long, cruel blade.

Something in-between sword and knife.

Black steel, curved forward in crescents and inlaid with red jewels. Some jewels missing, the weapons once-beautiful but now nicked and scratched from frequent, heavy use. The blades were chipped in places, although The Princess imagined

WON'T ABANDON. YET NOW BEGINS THE TALE
ESCAPE FROM THE
TAKEN AWAY FROM
YOU CAN NOW
THE DRAGON!
NO ONE WILL NOTICE IF YOU RUN AWAY!
START HERE
SAFE KEEPING
HIDE YOURSELF AWAY!
DEEP DESPAIR
OR

they must be sharp. He thought all of this through a haze, whatever drug he had been given still not quite shaken from his system.

In front of him, in this dungeon, claws upraised, the blackred Dragon.

She stepped forward, toward him.

She raised one curved blade, then patted at herself with the other, moaning.

He raised his bound hands to ward her off. She reached toward him with one hooked blade, poking at his stomach painfully, pushing him back. The other blade came up, and he struggled and swatted at her.

She withdrew, holding both talons wide. Moaned. Then she came again, hooking at his belly. First with one claw, then the other, seeming to play with him. He swatted at the knives, trying to push them away.

Then her prodding knife cut his stomach.

He shrieked and fought, which sent him swinging. Blood dripping to earth, toward his chest, from the shallow wound.

She cut him down.

The blades hacked a few times, cutting his leg twice — careless, shallow cuts — and sliced the ropes to drop The Princess, to thud him onto the plywood, which sagged under their weight.

His shoulder slammed the flooring while the Dragon watched. Her arms twitched, the blades jumping up between them. One she used to pat her own stomach, moaning through her mask.

Hungry.

She wanted him.

She wanted his blood. She wanted to open him with her blade.

Her eyes flickered over him. Her throat, beneath the mask, offered stifled, muffled roars.

He recovered a moment, rose to his feet, swayed. His head hurt, his leg hurt, his stomach hurt. He looked toward the door. She tensed and spread her arms. She twitched, writhed, her whole body wanting to launch itself at him.

But she was waiting.

In the air between them, sizzling, he could taste the pain she planned for him.

*

The Princess's mind started to come back to him as he felt her cruel black blades about to jump. He did not know the past but he could see his future. He considered the hallway beyond her, which led deeper into The Castle. The door behind him? That door must lead outside. But that wasn't the way she was guarding. It must be a false exit. He

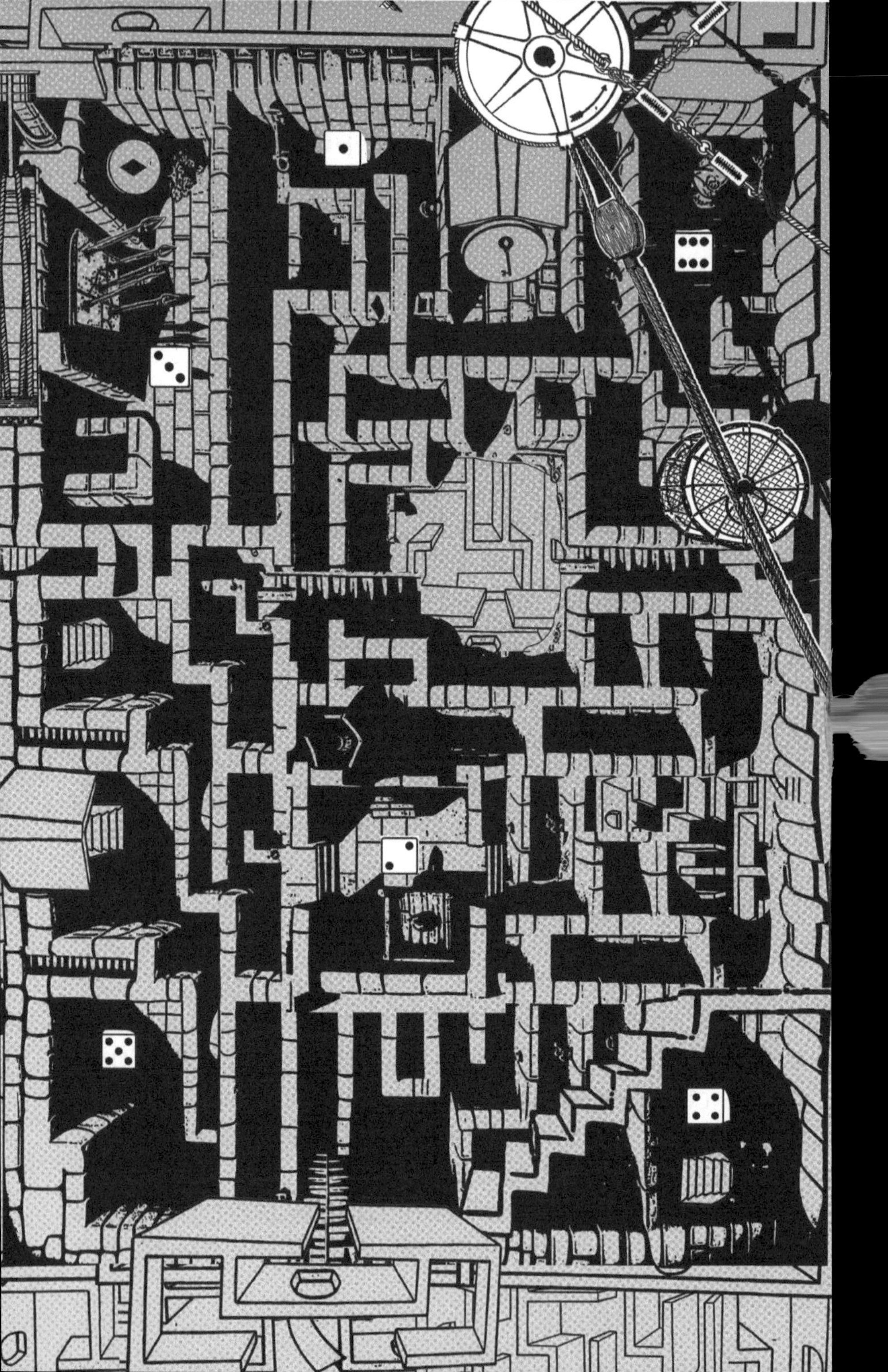

TOWER OF APPROVAL!
FINISH
Do you
NO ONE WILL
NOTICE IF YOU
RUN
AWAY!
DEEP
DESPAIR
feel lost in a maze of the story others tell about

reached down to pick up the Princess mask.

The Dragon froze, eyes tight to the mask.

The Princess held the mask between them. Turned its face toward The Dragon. Moved it left and right. Watched her follow it, watched her eyes stick tight to the mask's empty sockets as it swayed.

Then he screamed in fear and rage, throwing the mask toward the right. The Dragon still followed it with her eyes and he took that second to run past her. Toward the shadowed hall. Deeper into The Castle.

He crashed down the long dark hallway feeding out of the garage bay and deep into the recesses of the The Castle. This place had once been a medical facility of some kind. The hallway choked with gurneys and boxes of glassware. Walls painted an institution green, formica flooring worn from overuse, tiles missing to reveal lumpy epoxy underneath. Gaps where the green tiles lay shattered or missing, damaged scales on dragonhide.

Of course, The Dragon followed, blades biting at his heels.

The facility was dark but here and there signs and machines spoke of a forgotten world. The occasional emergency bulb offered a dim red spill of light. He rushed through the long hall, passing large metal

DEEP
DESPAIR
lost in a maze of the story others tell about you? Do unrealized expectations give you night
es a DRAGON chase you through your life? Maybe the STORYBOOK PROGRAM is right for you
SAFE KEEPING
HIDE YOURSELF AWAY!
OR
CHOOSE
YOUR

doors — he had not gained enough distance from her to risk stopping, turning, trying doors. The hallway split at its end and he took the left-hand path because he was left-handed — he had no logic, only instinct, only a bloodrush to survive.

This new hall led him crashing into a laboratory and he smashed into a desk, had to steady himself for a moment, lost some ground. He swept glass tubes and canisters onto the floor behind him as he rose, then kept tipping glass and anything else he could manage to reach as he ran — Bunsen burners, metal trays, anything that might hurt her trampling feet, slow her down, or cause her to slip. He did these things by instinct. Flung a mildewed carton of glass vials toward her and she swatted at it with both knives. He became filthy from the mildew and grease and dust of the abandoned space. Crashed through his new world and crashed what he could to the floor as The Dragon crashed after him, unstoppable, endless, a death that hurtled through space and time to find this moment and force him to receive her.

The Princess rushed through another door to enter a new hallway. An open elevator stood off to the side, some distance down. He decided to take the risk. He pushed his muscles further and rushed into it. Hammered the button to close it and the doors responded, even faster than he had hoped, a stroke of luck. But The Dragon was coming. He could see her pick up speed. He kept his finger on the button, ready to abort, ready to rush out and try to outrun her again. But the elevator seemed his best hope and she seemed just a moment too slow and he held his finger down and watched The Dragon run for him and raise her blades and closed his eyes to wait for her claws but nothing came.

Nothing came, not even the sound of The Dragon hitting the closed doors.

The Princess opened his eyes and saw metal before him, saw his finger on the button, realized that in his panic he had forgotten to choose a new floor.

Was she just outside, waiting? Or had she run elsewhere? He looked to the elevator controls and saw that The Castle was smaller than he had hoped. There were only three floors and a basement.

The Princess blinked. He did not know where he was now. Was he in the basement already? The room he had awoken in seemed like a garage bay, but it could have been at ground level or ramped down or up. He could be anywhere in the facility, really. He knew nothing but the world he woke into and that world was a disorienting terror

UNICORN
THE
Princess

THE
DRAGON

that had no up or down, no north or south, nothing but pursuit and blades.

They might be on any of the three floors, or in the basement, and if he pressed the button for the floor he was already on, then the elevator would not move. Its doors would simply open, and The Dragon would have him.

He held the close-door button and tried to listen for The Dragon. She was quiet, so quiet. Had she left? The longer he waited, the more time she had to move to another floor, to wait for him there. The more confusing the choice became.

The choice opened him to freedom or horror. Maybe he could stay here forever, in the cool steel of the elevator, between life and death, in the limbo before choice, refusing to move forward into his story.

But this was an Old Story, and it would not be denied. Another memory flashed back to him, that voice again:

"Three is a magic number."

He did not know what this meant, but the message was clear. He did not know if it could be trusted, but there were two of them, he reasoned, antagonist/protagonist, and so he pressed three to put some distance between those two, and closed his eyes and waited.

He waited until he felt the elevator

move.

It moved slow.

It moved slow.

It moved slow and he thought about the world, what it was now. What happened to the world? Had it always been this way? Had he simply never known but it had always been this way? A place built on Old Stories?

"The Old Stories must be told to keep The Book alive." That voice again, in his memory, the voice he could not remember. Whose voice? Was it his own? The Princess thought about speaking but was too afraid that it would be his voice.

The elevator doors opened and The Dragon flailed into the car. He had moved too slowly, thought too long, and she had overtaken The Princess using the stairs.

He snapped his head back, but she caught his cheek with the broken tip of one blade, gouging him. She swung again — she was in the car now, blocking his exit, but he was bigger and in this small place there was no room to swing with force. He grabbed her by the shirt front and slammed her as hard as he could, slammed her backward with all of his weight, all his strength, and she

whimpered. The hook-claws carved shallow ribbons across his back as she fought. They both fell, a tangle of kicks, and he tried to get out, get away, but she stabbed and flailed and he could not get away.

He had made a mistake getting into the elevator but so had she. He had realized his mistake but she had not. She was flashing her claws, crashing them into walls, seeking his skin his neck his blood, but she was rushing. This close, he could tell she was desperate, as desperate as he. The Dragon was desperate, panicked, radiating fear.

He lunged with two hands and trapped her left wrist. The Princess swung The Dragon's hand and fist hard against the ground, again and again, but she would not yield the blade. He could see her eyes, he could only see her eyes and they were filled with pain.

Her other claw hooked around his chest. And she pushed as hard as she could to get him off.

"Stop! Stop. Stop!"

A voice, finally, though it took a moment to recognize it as his own. He tumbled backward, out the elevator door, sprawling. His whole body raw and ragged and bloody from cuts, making the dirty floor under him slippery. He sobbed, crumpled, his strength fleeing. "Stop."

But she would never stop.

The Dragon rose, her back heaving up and down in great gasps. She pointed both knife tips down then pulled them up, towering over The Princess in the room's wavy light. The Dragon moved her claws outward, one to each side. Then pointed to him with one blade, moaning, patting her stomach with the other.

"Please, just stop."

"The Old Stories must be told to keep The Book alive." The voice in his memory kept returning, but it was not his voice, he knew that now. And The Dragon, he could see, had no voice.

The Princess looked around this new room. Trouble lights hung in a line down another hallway, the masonry of this hall in great disarray, only partially constructed, abandoned before its completion. Cinder blocks in tumbled stacks, an old trowel.

He screamed and threw the trowel with all his might. It hit her flat and fell away. His failure so spectacular he laughed.

She charged him then, dropping under his next swing, catching him in the chest with her shoulder. Hooked his legs with the knives and down they went, together again. As perhaps they were fated to be. He was under her this time, but the blades were too far apart to strike and he grabbed her face, getting purchase on the mask and a handful of her hair, and swung her head to the side and into the stacked cinder blocks.

The Dragon went limp for a moment and he thrust his hips up and flung her over. Still, she didn't let go of those infernal knives. She reached for his belly with them, again and again, but the thick leather cords wrapping his midsection kept him from being disemboweled when the points dug and stabbed.

The Princess fell away, twisting and landing in a huff. He grabbed a half-broken chunk of cinder block, the size of a loaf of bread, and lurched to his feet.

He spun, terrified to meet her, but she no longer faced him. Instead, The Dragon crawled at his feet, on all fours, scratching at the floor, furious. Putting her face down there as if trying to bite at something. She seemed to have forgotten him in her panicky clawing. She scrabbled at the ground and he watched her, stunned, confused, almost pitying her in her frantic desperation. But then he remembered his role, remembered that she was a monster, and he raised the broken cinder block over his head.

The Dragon turned toward him at the motion, her eyes wide. She raised both talons in protection, but was too slow, and he dropped the block onto her face.

The Dragon's mask did not tear but

her head changed shape. He brought the cinder block down on her again, and again, until the shape inside of her mask no longer looked like a human head. Driven down by these strikes, The Dragon lay spasming on the floor where she had just been scratching and biting. The weight of the cinder block buckled his tired muscles and he dropped it, falling forward in exhaustion, laying prone across her twitching form. Close enough then to see the thing she had been so intent on.

A number of leather cords that had bound and protected him, but been cut off, lay under her. Where the mass of cords stuck out, he saw something laced through their binding: a key. That was what made her chase him. That was what she had gouged at his stomach to get.

*

For a moment, he believed that the story was over. The Dragon lay at the feet of The Princess, awash in blood. Her one eye, still aligned with the eye hole, was open inside of the mask, lifeless, and The Princess felt instinctual pity for her, for this person, no longer The Dragon but some poor woman lying dead on a pile of bricks wrapped in blood.

"Three is a magic number."

He looked down at the woman lying broken in an unfinished room. "I'm not alone. An Old Story. A Dragon and a Princess, a Castle and a Prince."

He looked down at his own empty hands, then to her weapons. He needed her weapons. But she would not give up the blade.

Though her wrist was, he found, broken, though she was dead, she would still not give up the blade.

He looked more closely at her hand. It wrapped the handle of the sword and he tried to pull the fingers off one by one. But they would not come, they would not loosen. Something was wrong. They were stuck to the blade. Her skin was scarred by something toxic. Somebody had glued the weapons into her hands.

He raised his own hands to her mask.

What remained of her dead, dull eye stared through him as he rolled up the mask, rolled it over her chin, exposed her mouth.

Now he knew why she could not talk, why she never screamed. Her lips were melted together, her whole mouth a scar, the flesh burned shut. In effect, she had no mouth, just trauma and flesh where a mouth should be.

*

The world let him believe that he was free. The world allowed him to reenter the elevator, to take it to the ground floor. The world let him walk back through the broken hallways, filled with the traces of her pursuit, let him step over smashed glass and splayed metal, let him return to the garage bay once more. Now though, with his experience as a guide, he could tell that other chases had occurred here. So when he returned to the garage bay he was half-expecting what he found.

There hung another Princess.

He stared up at the body, hung upside-down like he had been. She was beautiful. Long blonde hair hung to the floor and pooled beneath her drugged face, slack and peaceful. Her legs were tied separately, so that they spread apart, and her hands hung past her face, her whole body limp.

Behind her, blocking the exit door, stood six others. Wrapped in white suits and hoods, faces covered wholly by cloth, but The Princess knew that they could somehow see him.

He turned to run again but six others stood behind him now, blocking the hall. They had come quietly, somehow, from hidden places. Had been there all along. Watching.

He looked back and forth between the two rows of hooded figures, unsure, uncertain. Before him hung a woman, blonde and drugged and happy in her dream. Between one world and the next stood twelve white cloaks.

Then between the cloaks, from out of the heart of the facility's darkness, stepped a man. Naked, long and lithe, white skin blacked over with ink. The inked man stopped just a few feet away. The Princess wished he had The Dragon's blades. The inked man tilted his head, just a tiny bit, and watched him with his bright and too-wide eyes.

Somehow, he knew that this man was a Book.

The others were its Pages.

Then the Book spoke and its voice was like the beginning of a storm, a tinkling rain of glass.

"You were the world's one treasure, but now you have outgrown that skin." It spread its hands wide, to indicate its Pages.

The Book offered him a simple, sad, small smile. Its tone tried to be hopeful. "May your second skin suit your flesh better."

Then the Pages fell upon him and the

world ended again.

*

The Dragon stood before The Princess, claws bared.

He watched her sleep. The peaceful sleep of limbo. In the darkness between worlds. He envied her. Soon she would wake into this world, into The Castle, into an Old Story.

When she woke he would give her a moment, to open her eyes. To open her eyes to his world. She would open her eyes, then he would cut her down. He would cut her down and wait to see what she would do.

He would wait, because that was the Story.

He would wait, torn between pages.

On one page, she ran. She ran and so he chased her, because The Dragon took The Princess. She was his treasure. He had claws only for her. He would cut out her key, cut her to pieces if he must. He would have his freedom.

On the other page, she came to kiss him. If she came to kiss him, then he would become a Prince. He would kneel before his

Princess. In his mouth the acrid metal taste of his own key, locked in its hiding place. If she kissed him, he would cut open his mouth, cut the key out for her, Prince that he was, he would sacrifice himself to save her.

Whose key would find the door? Which secret would be cut out? Which story would be told?

He waited, twitching in frustration, in fear, wanting to tell her how this Story should go. Wanting to offer her the safety of the second page. But he could not speak. Dragons do not speak. They breath fire, melt their mouths shut.

This was an Old Story. A frightful, ancient story, one told time and again, one that waited for an ending.

But the ending never came

and so

never died.

Dr. Storybook's
STORYBOOK PROGRAM
EVALUATION
AND PRESCRIPTION!
Pick the kind of STORY YOU WANT
Do you suffer from the unrealized expectations of others?
When waiting, do you get mad moments before the person shows up?
Do you suffer from a nightmare where you are pursued by a killer ?
Do you delight in dreams where you pursue others?
Have you ever had a nightmare?
Princess
Dragon
APPROVED
Princess
Dragon
We think you are perfect for the STORYBOOK PROGRAM
Storybook
TELL US YOUR NIGHTMARE!
1-888-53-STORY
(1-888-537-8679) TOLL FREE!
LIFE
IS NOT
A
FAIRY TALE

A road within
yourself unfolds
The Path
you won't abandon.
Yet now begins
your tale untold...
THE
Princess
AND THE
DRAGON

"A road within
yourself unfolds,
The path you
won't abandon.

Yet now begins
your tale untold,

The PRINCESS
and
The DRAGON."

DISCARDED
ARMFUL

A road within
yourself unfolds

The Path
you won't abandon.

Yet now begins
your tale untold...

HARMFUL

The PRINCESS came
to Castle Keep;
In every room a jewel.
To Crown the Past
and wake from sleep;
this coronation
was a duel.

The dark within,
a grave concern.

Yet from despair you
must adjourn.

If Lighted Path
you may discern.

Within us all
The DRAGON asks;

Can you be brave,
in Castle Vast,

be bold, be fast,
complete each task?

This tale would
have you

Choose your mask.

Bereft a life of ease
and pleasure.

Now brave the maze
which takes your
measure,

to find The
KNIGHT and win
your treasure.

The DRAGON
is a long-cast shadow,

who follows always,
close with woe.

A *rage within*
that's never far,

from where
your
fleeing

footsteps go.

Heart beat, heart beat,
in your breast.

Twists and turns.
Unlock the chest.

Yield the gift
to guide your quest.

The DRAGON comes.

There is no rest.

I
II
V
XIII

To wake at last
from this dread slumber;

Where you
have been before.

There are here
a very careful
NUMBER

O' ways to
open up the door.

Within the secrets
there recorded,

a tool to escape
your trial.

But to find such
truth afforded,

you must defeat
the Wizard's dial.

These trees,
too quiet, do no good.

The Wizard's hand
remains unseen.

A crafted false
and silent wood

that conceals
his strange machine.

We oftimes will share
our stories,

a collection of our lies,

which lift us up to
unseen glories

as if their teller
never dies.

We all want to
ease the pressure

of many things
we can't let go.

Here within
The DRAGON's shelter,

Can you let a
Trapped Breath flow?

Though mercy
begs you hear the plea,

like a serpent
in the garden.

You know at last
you have a key;

there can be no bargain.

A road within
yourself unfolds
The path you
won't abandon...

LIFE
IS NOT
A
FAIRY TALE

Yet now begins
your tale untold;
The PRINCESS
and
The DRAGON.

A STORYBOOK PROGRAM ACTIVITY BOOK

THE Princess AND THE Dragon

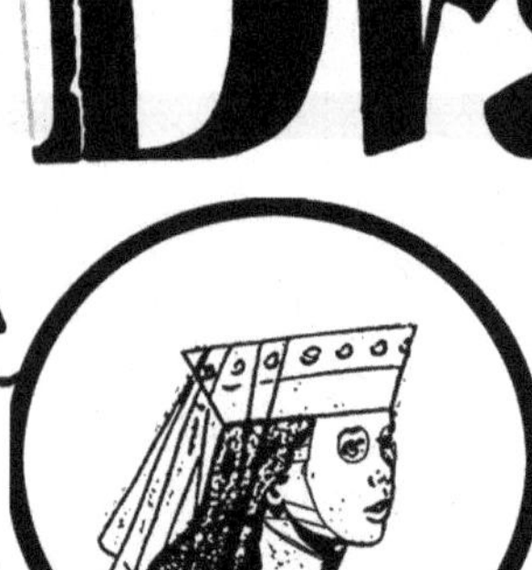

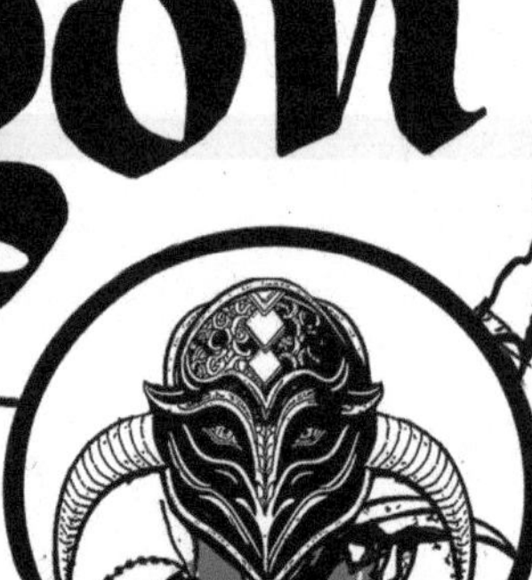

WHEN WE KNOW
WHO WE ARE
WE GET BETTER!

MINI GAME!

The Princess and the Dragon

FINISH

START

ESCAPE FROM THE FAIRY TALE

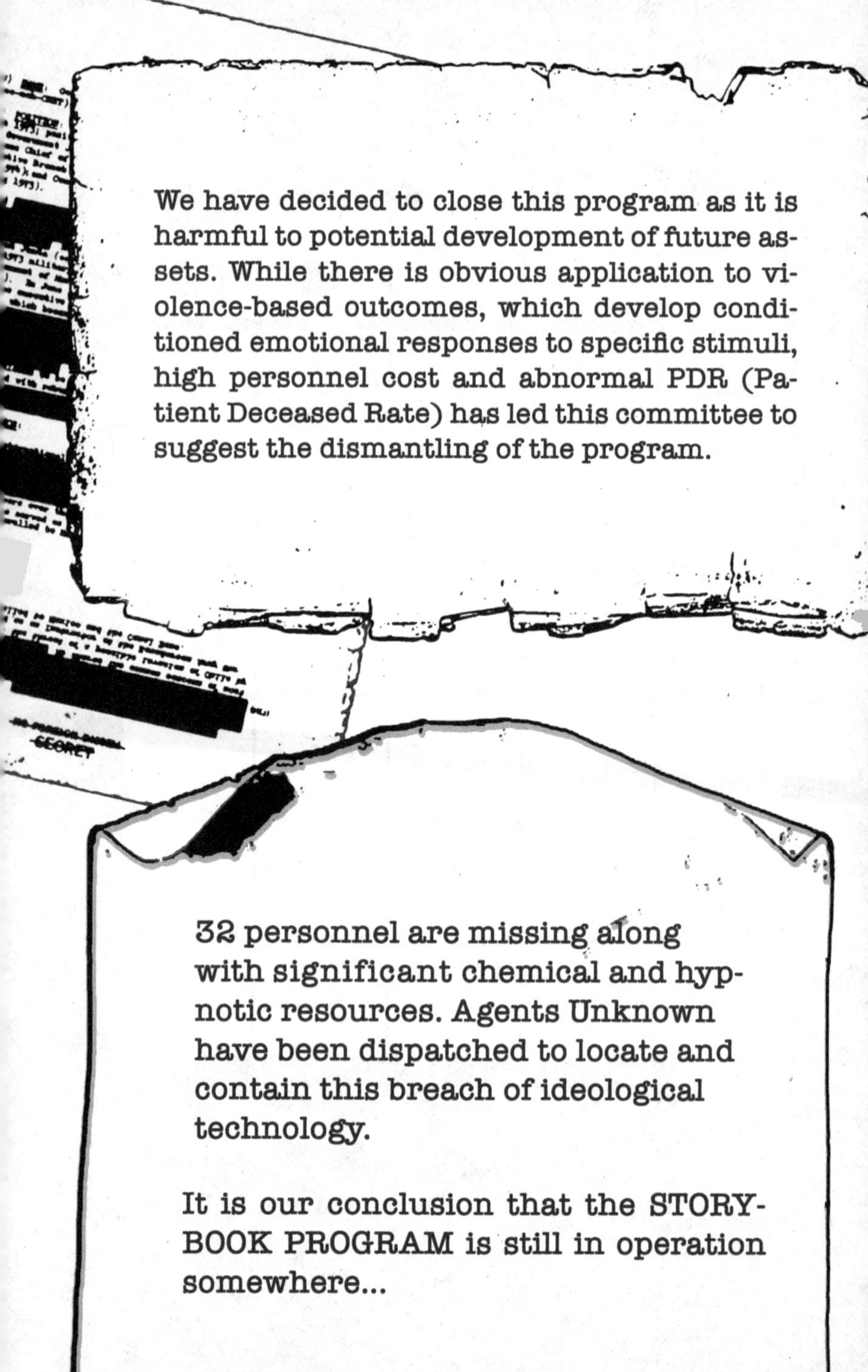
We have decided to close this program as it is harmful to potential development of future assets. While there is obvious application to violence-based outcomes, which develop conditioned emotional responses to specific stimuli, high personnel cost and abnormal PDR (Patient Deceased Rate) has led this committee to suggest the dismantling of the program.
32 personnel are missing along with significant chemical and hypnotic resources. Agents Unknown have been dispatched to locate and contain this breach of ideological technology.
It is our conclusion that the STORYBOOK PROGRAM is still in operation somewhere...

HARMFUL

the Storybook PROGRAM

We believe that "Dr. Storybook" is now operating a program recruiting from the general population.

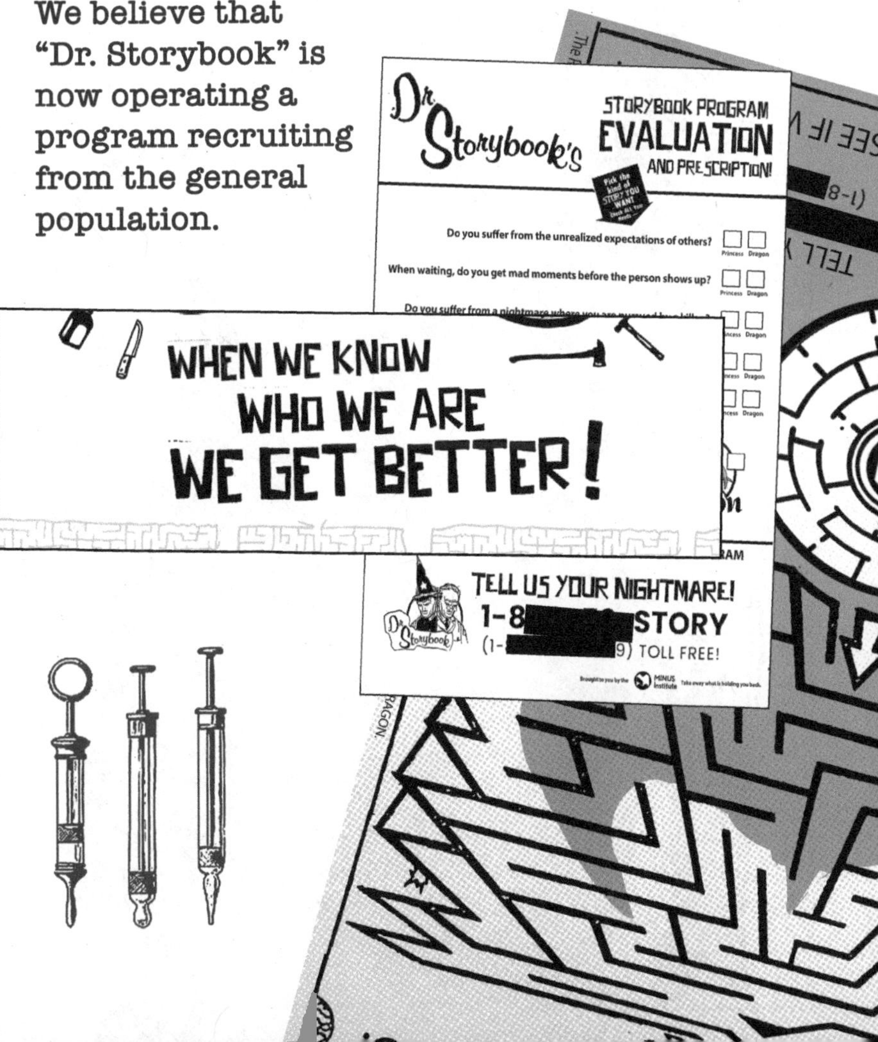

Significant physical evidence has been collected at multiple sites. They are indicative of Storybook Program treatment protocols. Though evidence does suggest some increasingly extreme developing pathology that diverges from original methodology.

The staff of the Storybook Program seem to have been inculcated with their own ideological framework.

They too perhaps, have been subsumed by their archetypes.

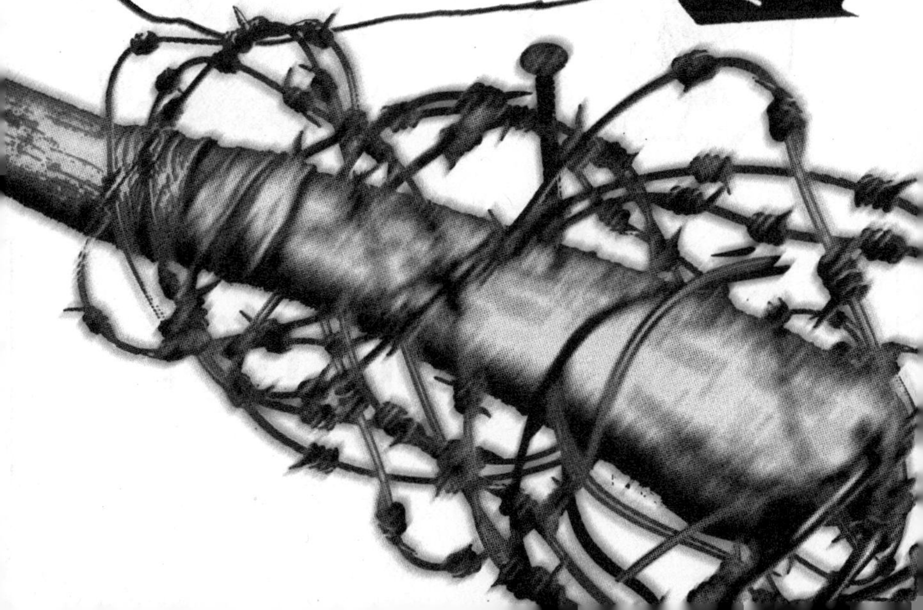

A STORYBOOK PROGRAM ACTIVITY BOOK

THE Princess AND THE Dragon

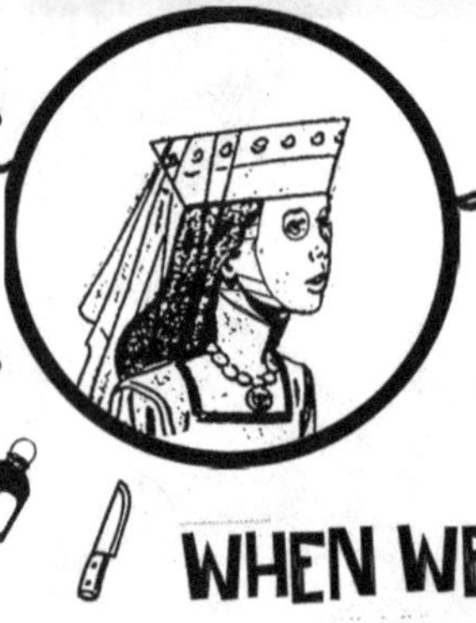

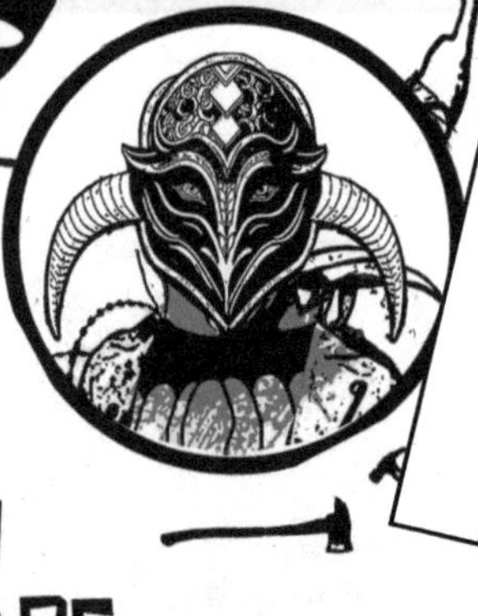

WHEN WE KNOW
WHO WE ARE
WE GET BETTER!

Dr Storybook
STORYBOOK PROGRAM
3 PLAYER GAME
"DR. STORYBOOK BELIEVES THAT IN EACH OF US ARE THE PRINCESS AND THE DRAGON.
IF WE KNEW OURSELVES BETTER - WE WOULD GET BETTER.
DR. STORYBOOK WANTS YOU TO BE THE PERSON YOU ARE MEANT TO BE ..."
Dr STORYBOOK/ THE WIZARD describes the clues and traps of the FAIRY TALE to help two patients get better. Flip a coin to see who your patients start as. THE PRINCESS tries to ESCAPE before THE DRAGON can catch them.
Suffering brings clarity.
FACE YOUR PERIL
Smashes
Bullets
Clues
Keys
Cuts
ROLL to BEGIN. Whenever the DRAGON + PRINCESS are in the same place they must FACE PERIL or RUN AWAY.
BOTH begin with SMASHES, CLUES and CUTS but BULLETS and KEYS must be introduced by Dr Storybook. TWO keys that make ONE are needed to open the INSIDE DOOR.
In a dispute between Patients Dr. Storybook decides.
Fail and lose a heart. If you LOSE HEART three times, you lose everything...
OR
RUN AWAY
+
GET LOST IN A LABYRINTH FIND YOURSELF
ncess
OUS and BRAVE.
Dragon
DRIVEN, HURT and BRUTAL.
forces,
noteworthy events.
-- INF response: Start of
bases following Andropov's announcement on 24 November
1983 of termination of the 20-month moratorium on SS-20
deployments opposite NATO; initiation
and Czechoslovakia, and continued propaganda and active
measures against INF deployment.
-- Soviet exercises:

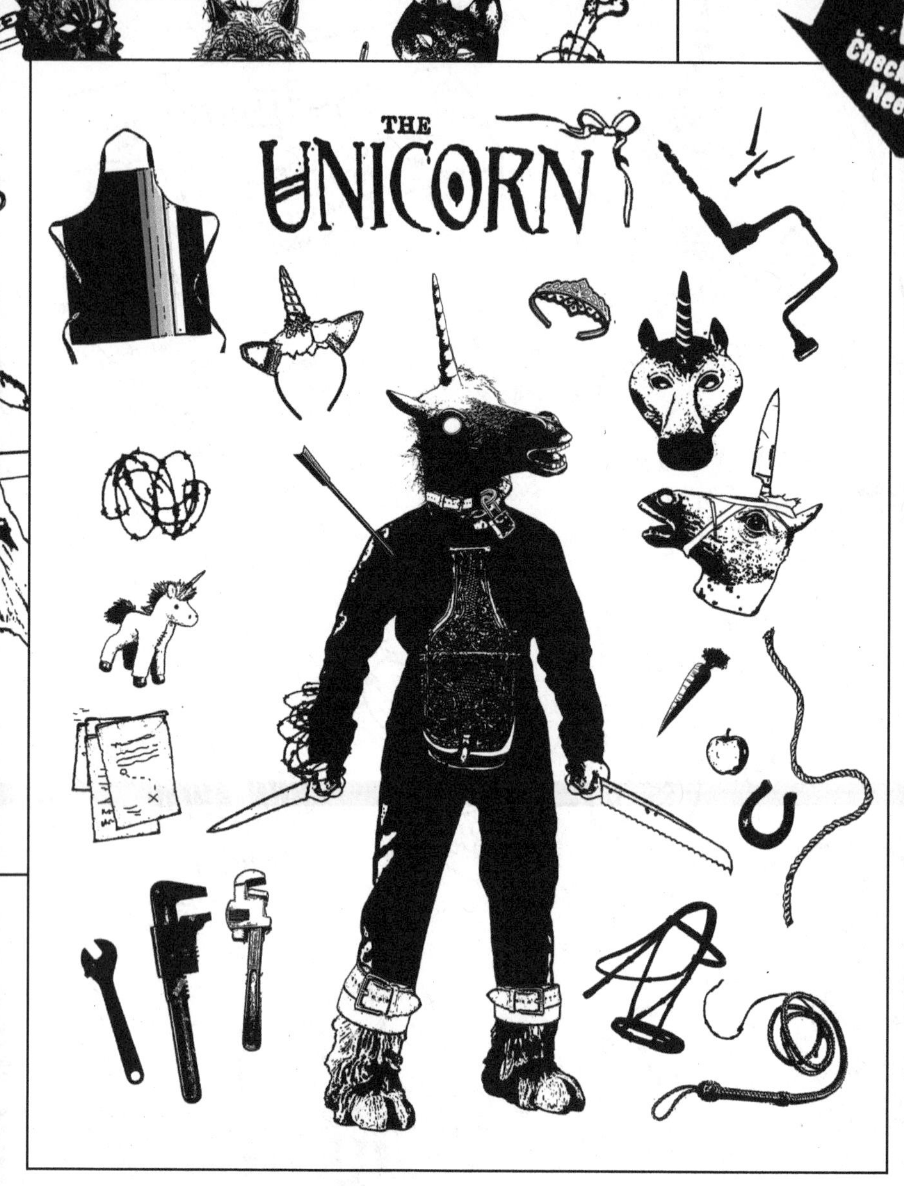

Alternative treatment archetypal projective elements have been discovered at many sites.

The Story is growing.

I AM
THE
Princess
OF
LIES FEARS DOUBTS
LOOKING FOR
Light STRENGTH TRUTH
TO ESCAPE DANGER
I RUN FOR MY LIFE!
I STAND AND FIGHT!
I HIDE AND STAY QUIET!
HIDDEN INSIDE IS
THE Dragon
THE UNICORN
THE Wolf
the Knight

START
THE Wizard
HAS TRAPPED YOU IN
THE MAZE THE DUNGEON THE WOODS
FILLED WITH
TRAPS! PHANTOMS! SCREAMS!
NIGHTMARES! SHADOWS!
YOU HAVE A
?
THE Dragon THE Wolf
THE UNICORN the Knight
IS FOLLOWING YOU.
HOW DO YOU GET AWAY !?!

THE
Princess

Pick the kind of STORY YOU WANT
Check ALL Your Needs —
I AM
THE Princess
OF
LIES FEARS DOUBTS
LOOKING FOR
Light STRENGTH TRUTH
TO ESCAPE DANGER
I RUN FOR MY LIFE!
I STAND AND FIGHT!
I HIDE AND STAY QUIET!
HIDDEN INSIDE IS
THE Dragon
THE UNICORN
THE Wolf
the Knight

THE DRAGON

START
Pick the kind of STORY YOU WANT
Check ALL Your Needs —
THE Wizard
HAS TRAPPED YOU IN
THE MAZE THE DUNGEON THE WOODS
FILLED WITH
TRAPS! PHANTOMS! SCREAMS!
NIGHTMARES! SHADOWS!
YOU HAVE A
?
THE Dragon THE Wolf
THE UNICORN the Knight
IS FOLLOWING YOU.
HOW DO YOU GET AWAY !?!

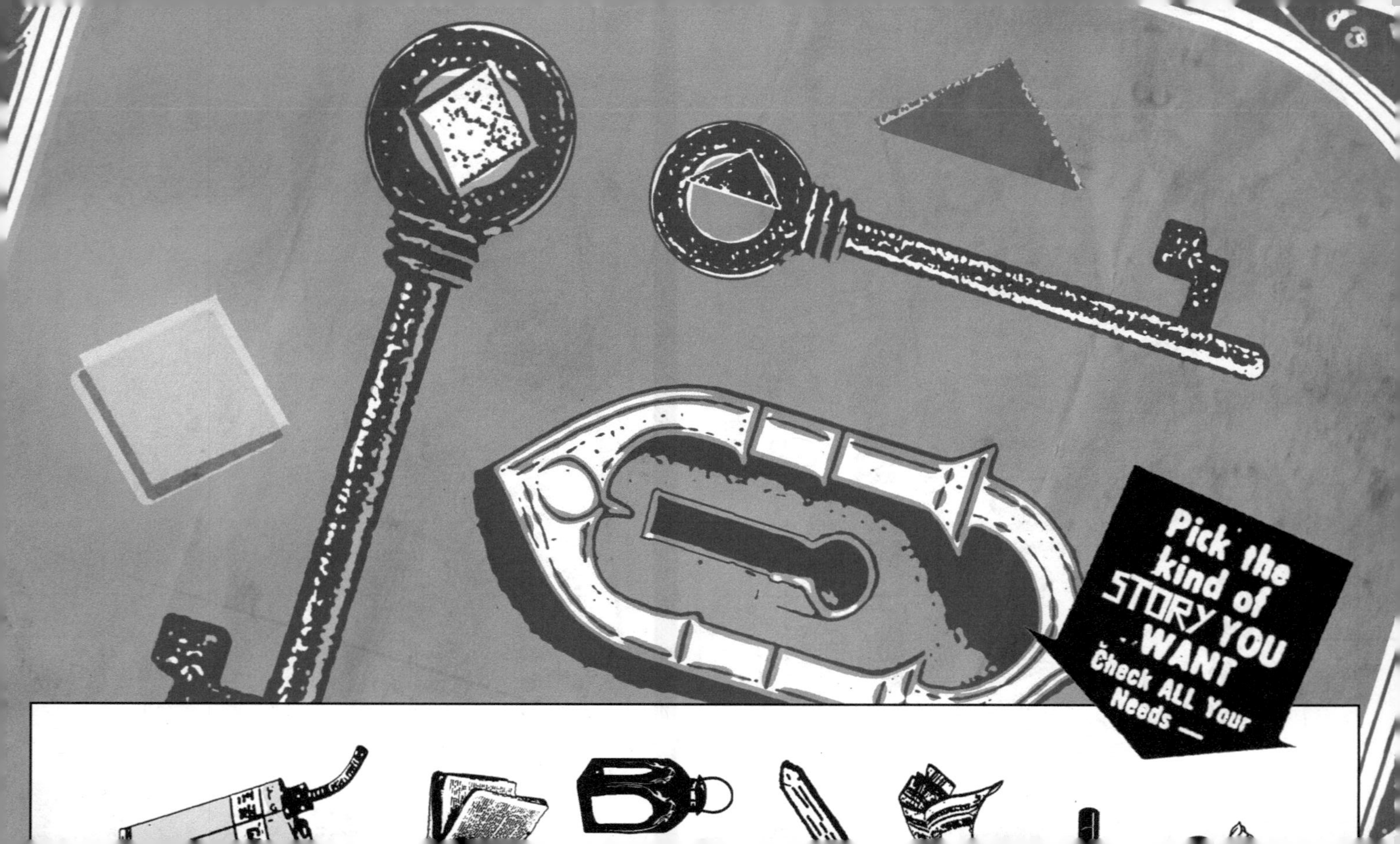
Pick the kind of STORY YOU WANT
Check ALL Your Needs —

the Knight

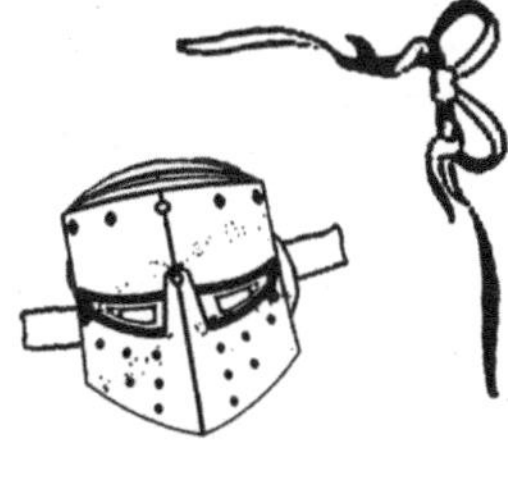

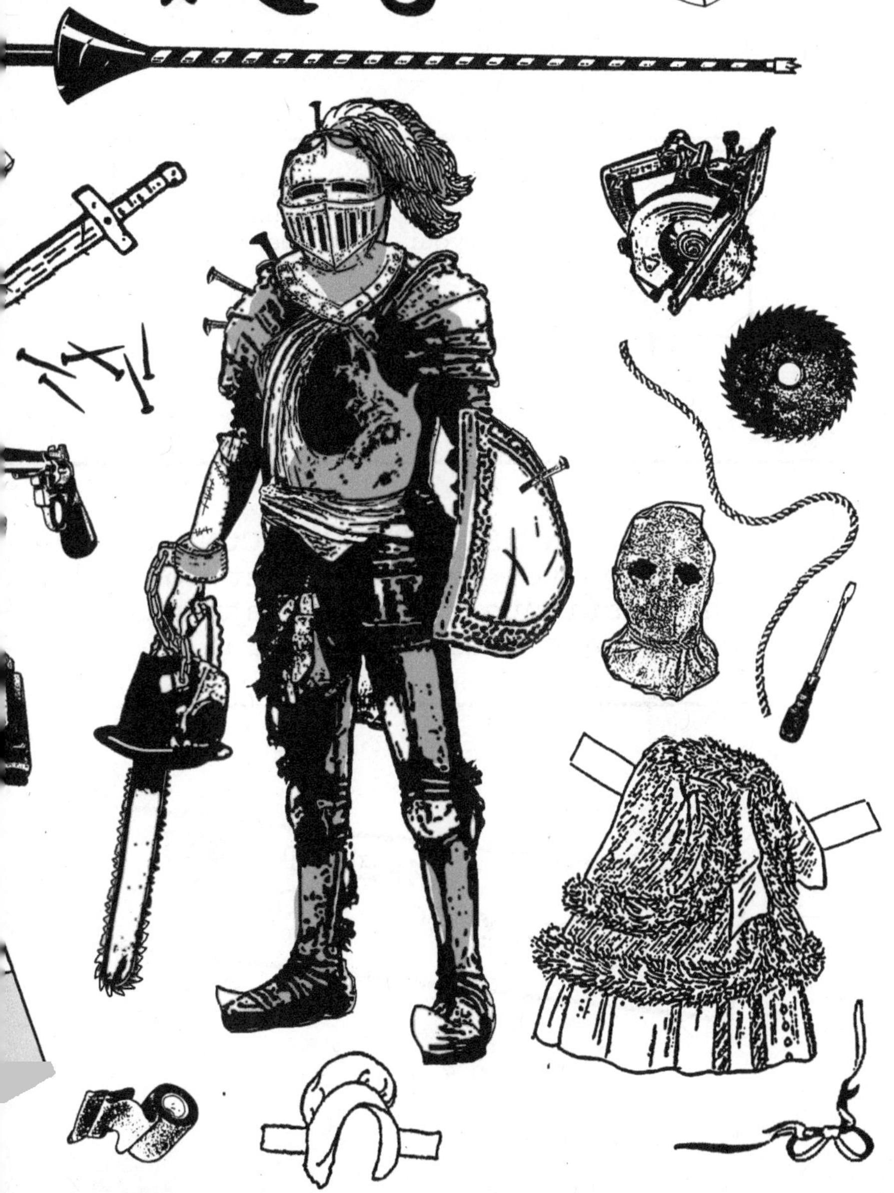

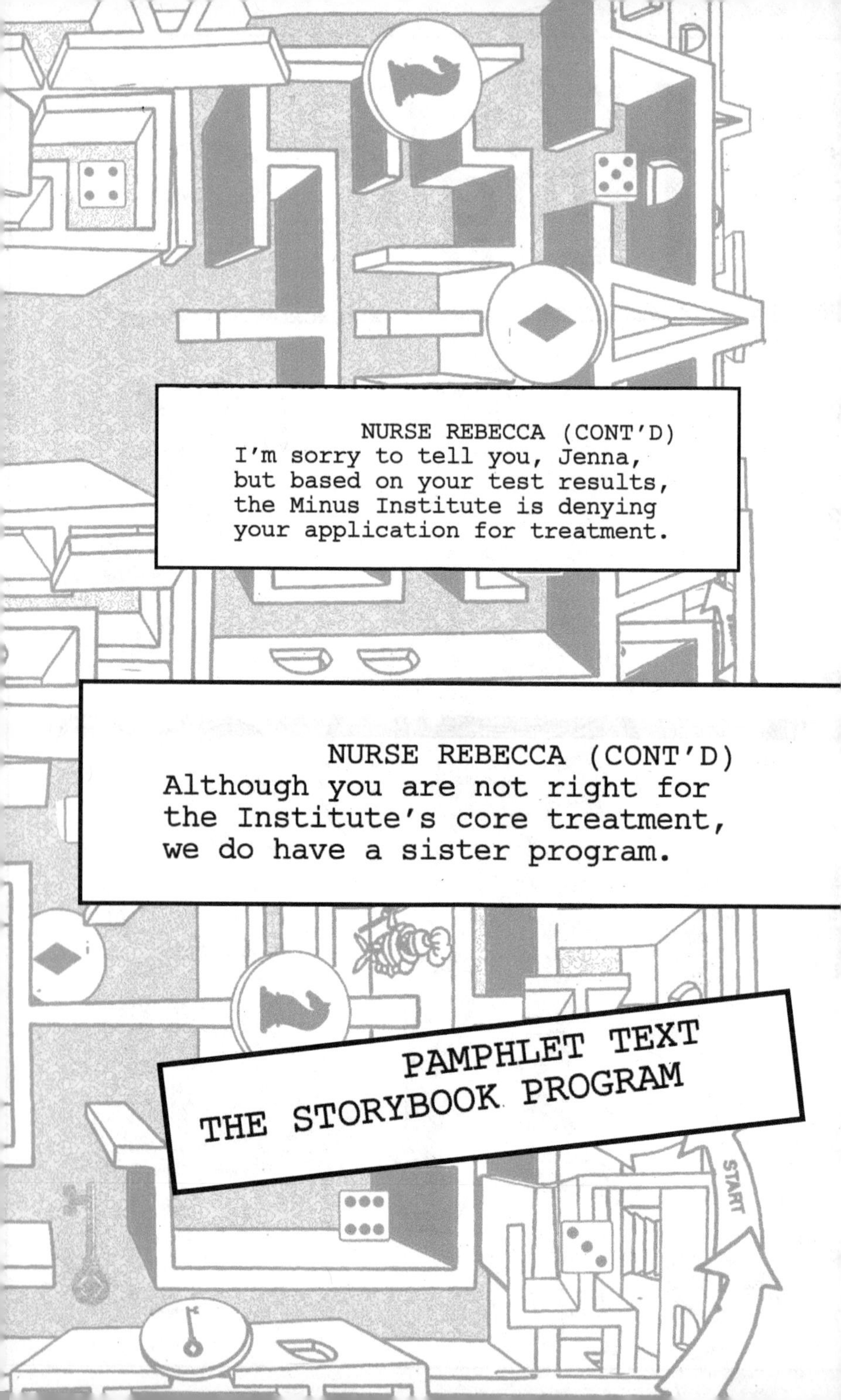
NURSE REBECCA (CONT'D)
I'm sorry to tell you, Jenna, but based on your test results, the Minus Institute is denying your application for treatment.
NURSE REBECCA (CONT'D)
Although you are not right for the Institute's core treatment, we do have a sister program.
PAMPHLET TEXT
THE STORYBOOK PROGRAM
START

WHICH WAY?
Can you help
the
Princess
Escape the
Fairy Tale?
the way out...
... is within.
FREE
Tremendous Surprise
Do you feel lost in a maze of the story others tell about you?
Do unrealized expectations give you nightmares?
Does a DRAGON chase you through your life?
Maybe the STORYBOOK PROGRAM is right for you?
TELL YOUR OWN STORY
1-888-53-STORY
(1-888-537-8679) TOLL FREE!
TELL US YOUR NIGHTMARES TO SEE IF WE CAN HELP.
The ROAD within yourself unfolds. The path you won't abandon. Yet now begins the tale untold, THE PRINCESS and THE DRAGON.

the Storybook PROGRAM

“The Storybook Program is both a physical maze and a conceptual labyrinth at the same time...”

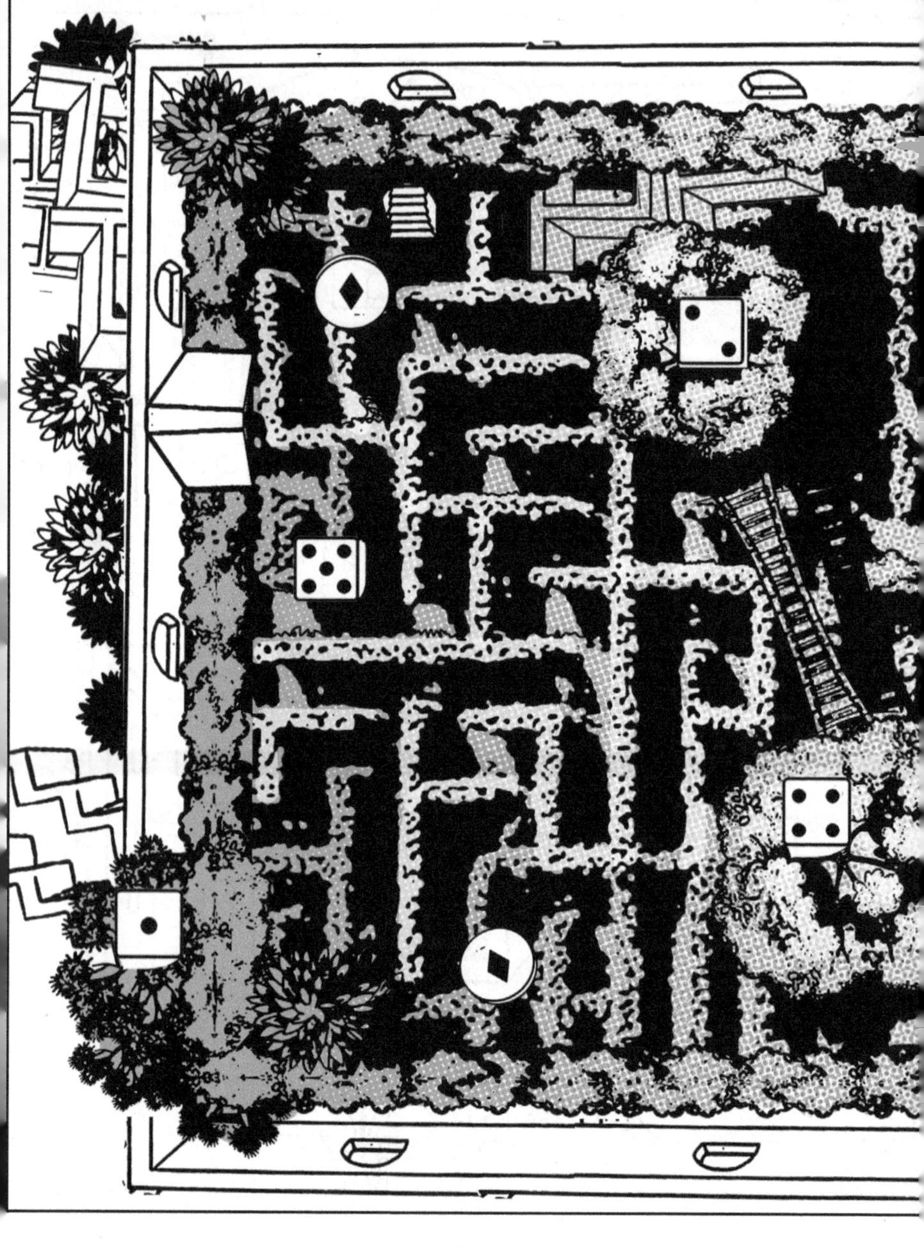

the Storybook PROGRAM

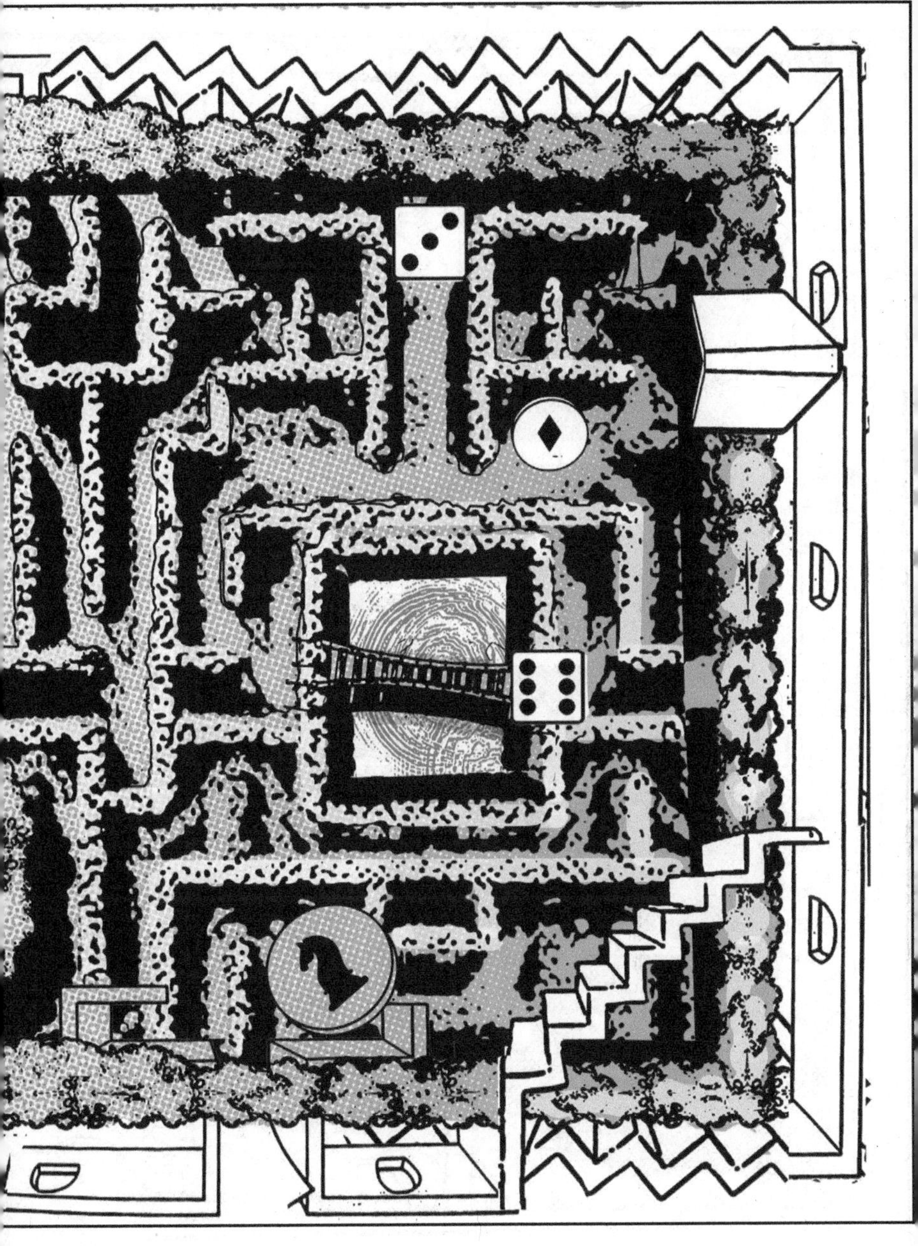

“A maze and a labyrinth are different.”

“A maze has dead ends. In a labyrinth, you’ll either end up free or at the centre.”

the Storybook PROGRAM

“To escape a Storybook Program you must always take the Sinister Path, avoid Dead Ends and Find Your Centre...”

THE ROAD WITHIN YOURSELF UNFOLDS. THE PATH YOU WON'T ABANDON. YET NOW BEGINS THE TALE UNTOLD. THE PRINCESS AND THE DRAGON.
Dr. Storybook
ESCAPE FROM THE FAIRY TALE
TAKEN AWAY FROM THE REAL WORLD
YOU CAN NOW CHOOSE WHO TO BE...
THE PRINCESS!
START HERE
THE DRAGON!

TOWER OF
FINISH
AWAY!
SAFE KEEPING
HIDE YOURSELF AWAY!
OR
DEEP DESPAIR
CHOOSE YOUR SELF
TELL YOUR OWN STORY
1-888-53-STORY
(1-888-537-8679) TOLL FREE!
Do you feel lost in a maze of the story others tell about you? Do unrealized expectations give you nightmares?
Does a DRAGON chase you through your life? Maybe the STORYBOOK PROGRAM is right for you?

THE PRINCESS & THE DRAGON

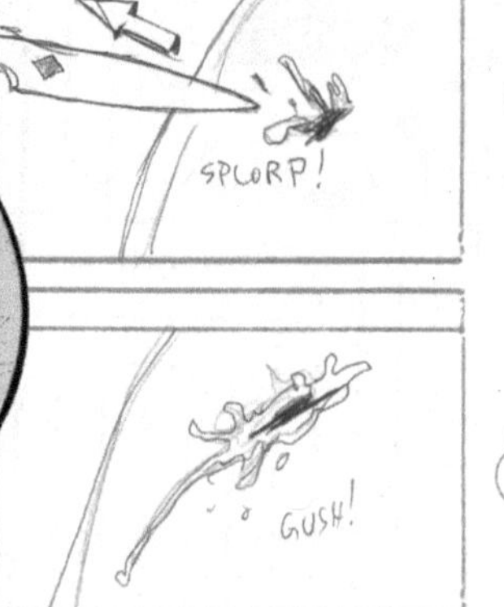

"...delusions of grandeur..."

"...all men dream but not equally..."

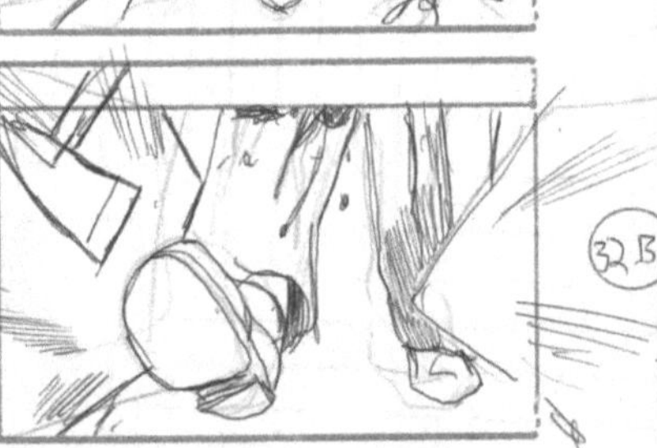

"Jenna?"

"Are you in there?"

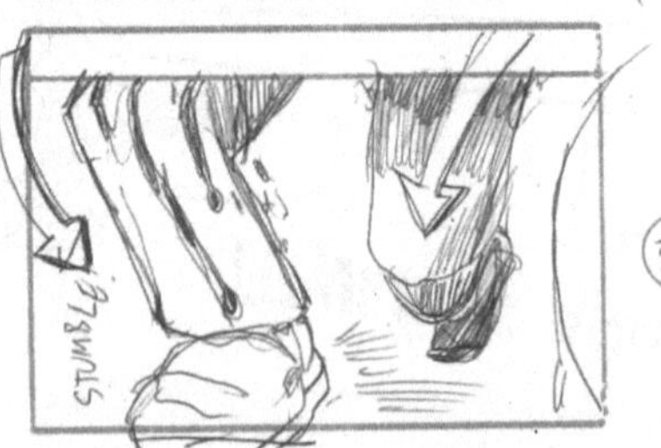

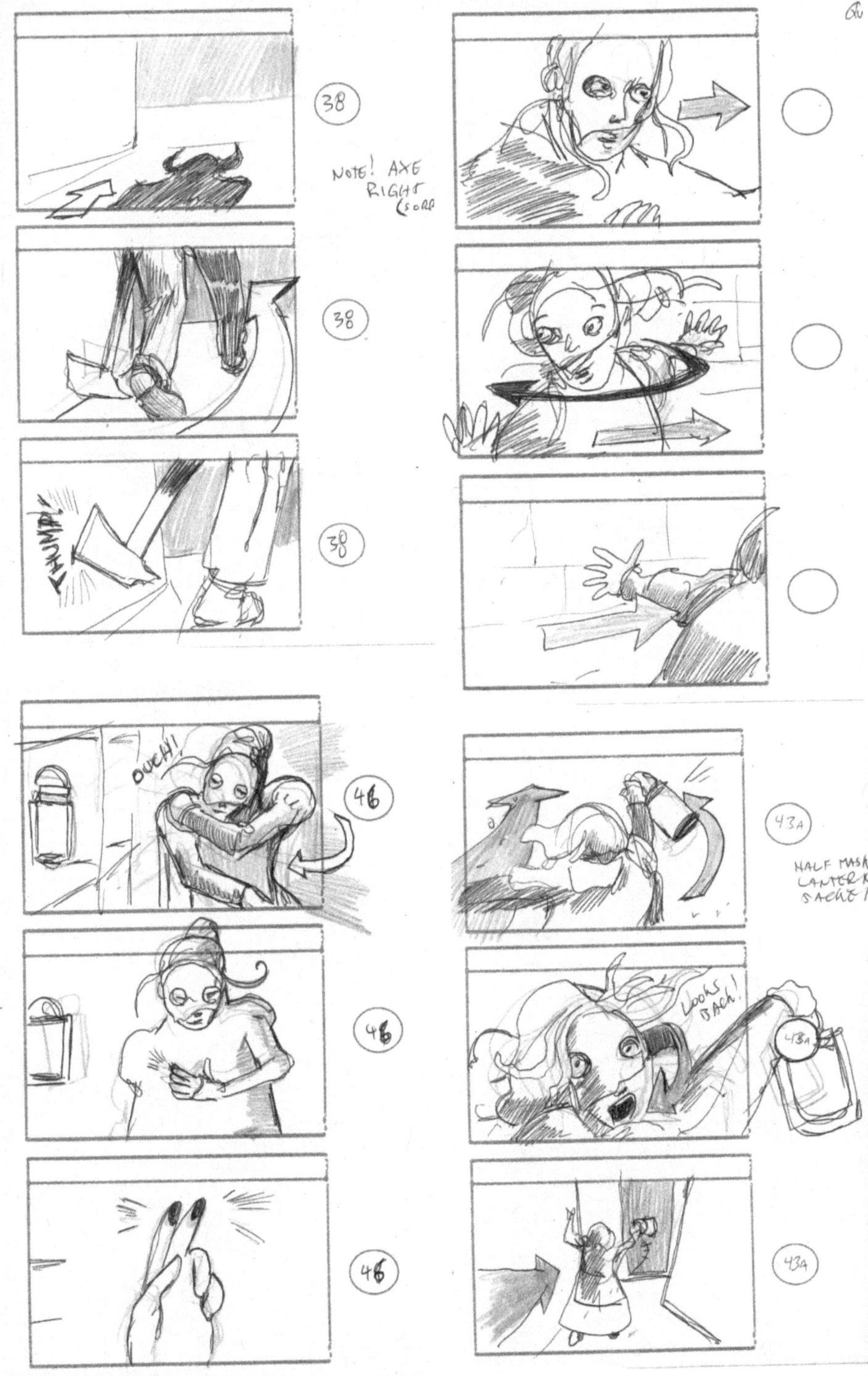

38
NOTE! AXE RIGHT (SORR
38
THUMP!
38
OUCH!
43A
HALF MASK LANTERN SACHE!
LOOKS BACK!
43A
43A

Half Mask
lantern
44A
44A
PUSH
44A
44B
44B
CRASH
44B
44C
44C
44C
43A
HALF MASK
Looks BACK!
43A
43A

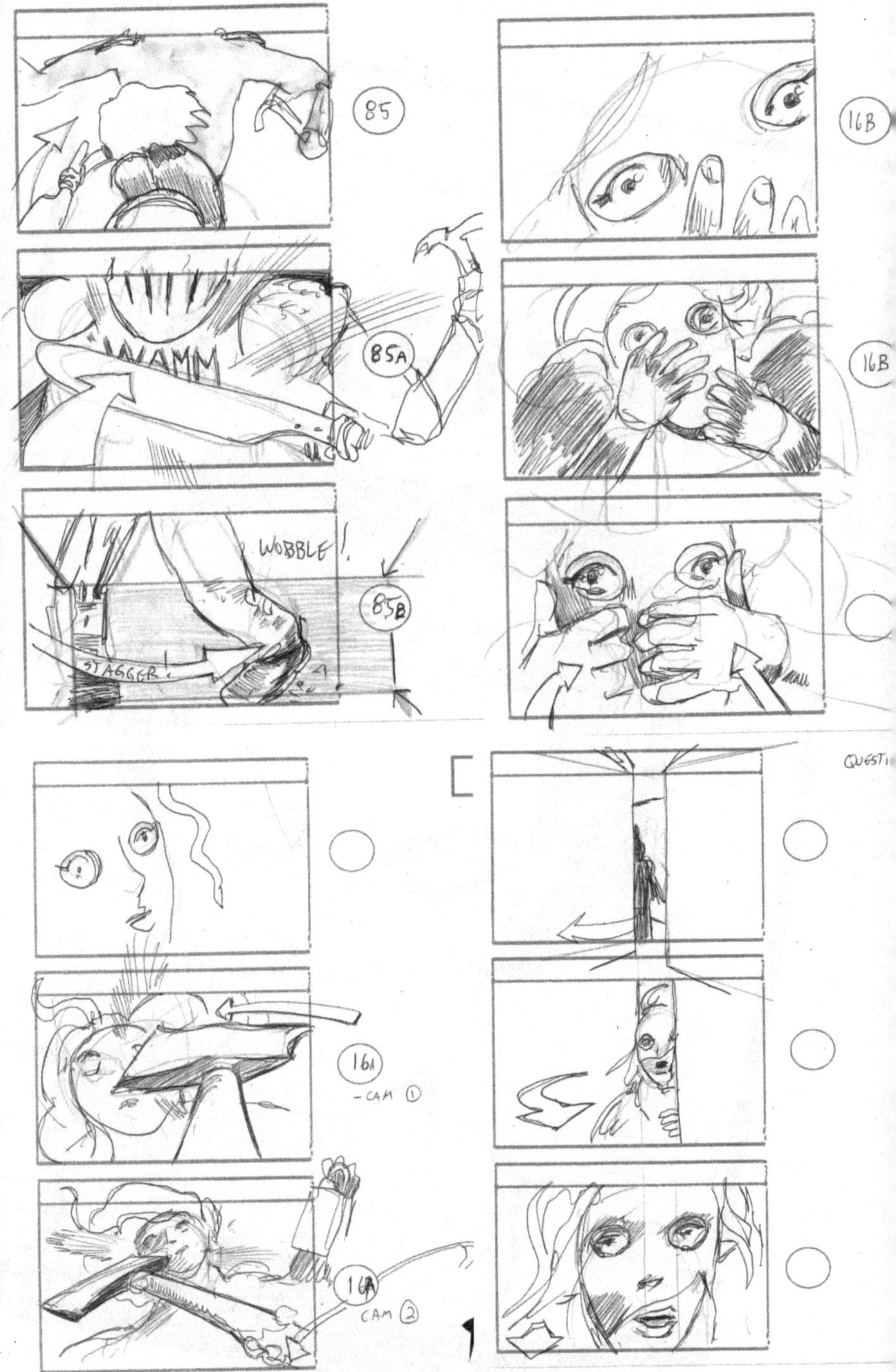
85
16B
WAMM
85A
16B
WOBBLE!
STAGGER!
85B
QUESTI
16A
-CAM ①
16A
CAM ②

THE WAY OUT IS WITHIN
OUTWARD ACTION REQUIRES INWARD MOTION
IT'S THE THOUGHT THAT COUNTS
It's time to get moving.

TAKE AWAY WHAT IS HOLDING YOU BACK

MINUS
Institute

BE BRAVE.

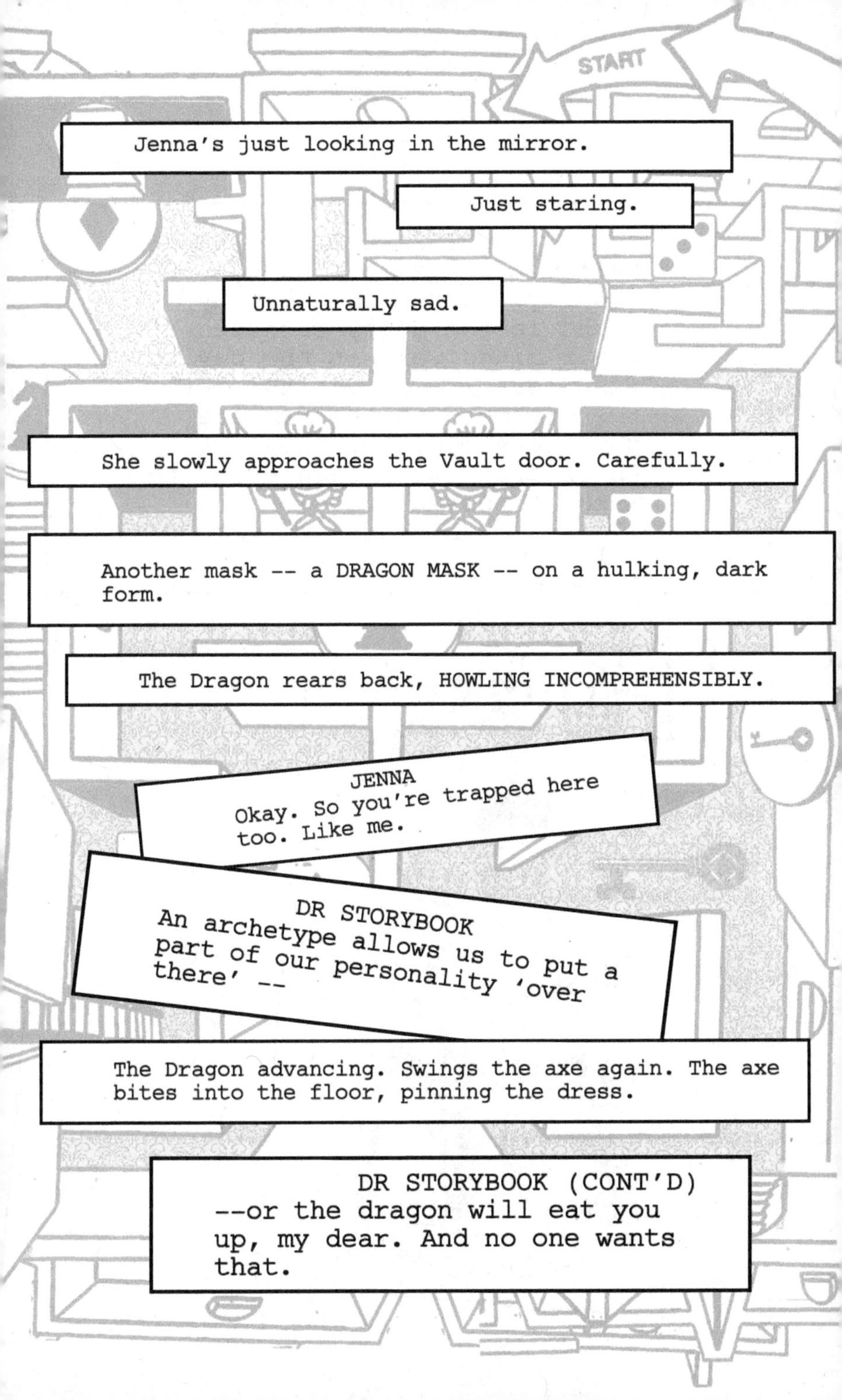
START
Jenna's just looking in the mirror.
Just staring.
Unnaturally sad.
She slowly approaches the Vault door. Carefully.
Another mask -- a DRAGON MASK -- on a hulking, dark form.
The Dragon rears back, HOWLING INCOMPREHENSIBLY.
JENNA
Okay. So you're trapped here too. Like me.
DR STORYBOOK
An archetype allows us to put a part of our personality 'over there' --
The Dragon advancing. Swings the axe again. The axe bites into the floor, pinning the dress.
DR STORYBOOK (CONT'D)
--or the dragon will eat you up, my dear. And no one wants that.

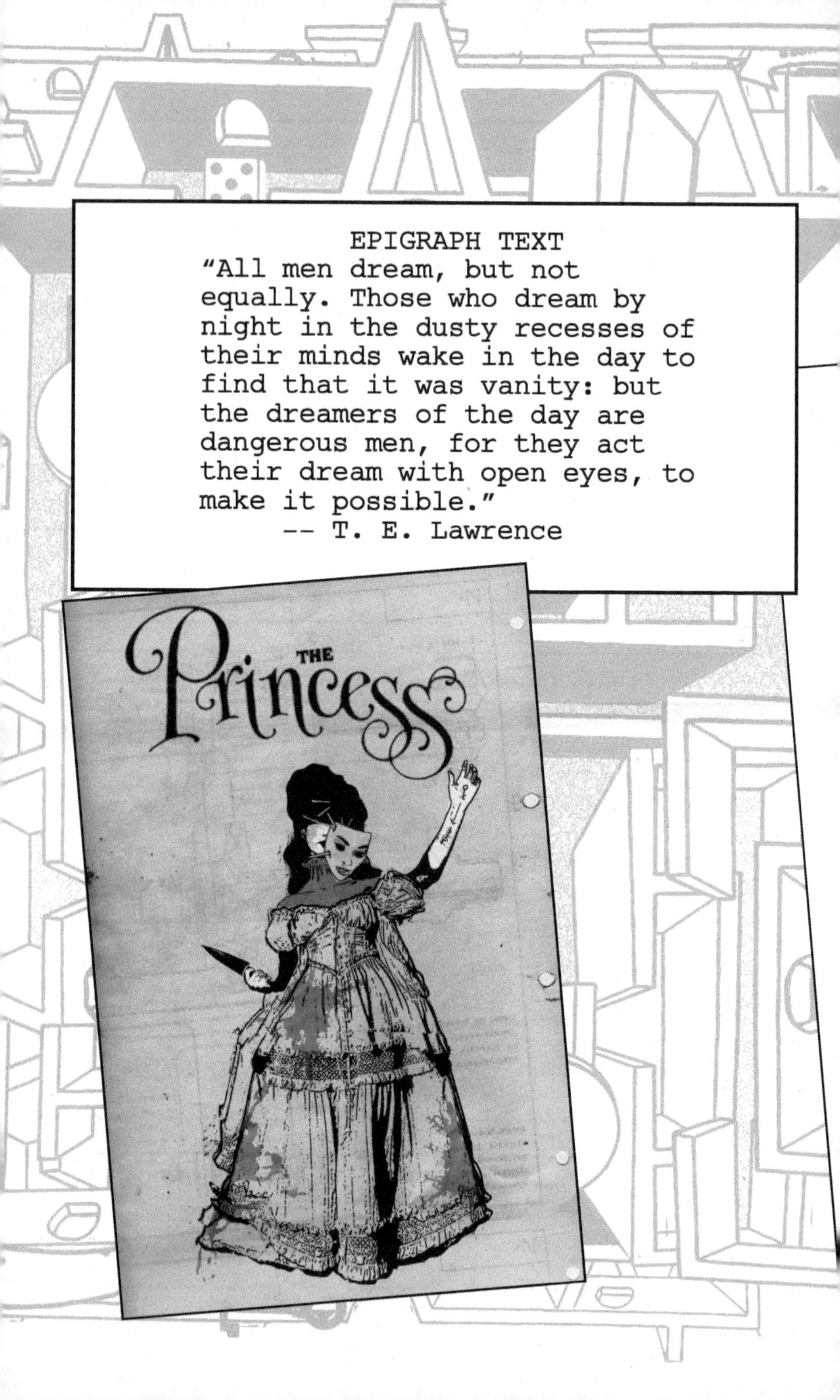
EPIGRAPH TEXT
"All men dream, but not equally. Those who dream by night in the dusty recesses of their minds wake in the day to find that it was vanity: but the dreamers of the day are dangerous men, for they act their dream with open eyes, to make it possible."
-- T. E. Lawrence
THE
Princess

THE PRINCESS & THE DRAGON

THE PRINCESS AND THE DRAGON

written by

GMB Chomichuk & Jonathan Ball

based on the short story by GMB Chomichuk & Jonathan Ball and including production notes based on location visit

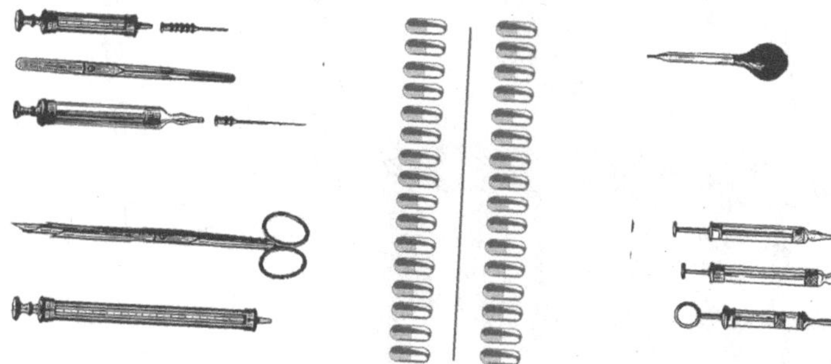

November 24, 2023

Are you tired of feeling like a mere puppet in life?
Break free from the shackles of doubt and indecision!
Don't miss this opportunity to rewrite your destiny.
Our cutting-edge brainwashing techniques will trans-
form you into a confident, unstoppable force.
THE
DRAGON
TAKE AWAY
WHAT IS
HOLDING YOU BACK

FADE IN

BLACK SCREEN

NOTE: This epigraph is present on-set at the location, so could be filmed, although it may look better as on-screen text. Maybe get a shot if only for "making-of" press materials since it's such a great part of the "story of" making this film.

An epigraph appears:

EPIGRAPH TEXT
"All men dream, but not equally. Those who dream by night in the dusty recesses of their minds wake in the day to find that it was vanity: but the dreamers of the day are dangerous men, for they act their dream with open eyes, to make it possible."
-- T. E. Lawrence

FADE OUT

TITLE CARD

NOTE: Title cards appear on screen as "storybook chapter headings" in a manner that recalls Pulp Fiction or Clerks but with an "evil storybook" stylization.

CHAPTER I

THE MINUS INSTITUTE

EXT. CLINIC DOORS - DAY

Large metal doors, like the gates of a castle.

INT. MINUS INSTITUTE WAITING ROOM - DAY

What seems like a hospital waiting room, or would, if the decor wasn't so weird.

INSERT POSTER

A Minus Institute poster on the waiting room wall.

The poster shows a man on a chair with smoke billowing above his head, a column of smoke like a hand reaching down and about to grab his head.

NOTE: Gregory has already made this poster so will provide the image and/or the physical poster.

POSTER TEXT
THINKING IS DANGEROUS.
(subhead)
Do you know where your ideas are coming from?
(logo)
MINUS Institute

BACK TO THE ROOM

Our eventual princess, JENNA, sits dejected in a chair in what looks like a hospital waiting room, except it's very narrow, with giant windows.

Jenna's looking at the poster. She turns to look at a BLACKBOARD in front of her.

INSERT BLACKBOARD

BLACKBOARD TEXT
1. Is your intake form complete?
(further down)
2. Have you listed ALL your medications?

START
THINKING IS DANGEROUS
Do you know where your ideas are coming from ?
MINUS Institute

BACK TO JENNA

Looking around still.

She sees another poster.

INSERT SECOND POSTER

NOTE: Gregory has already made this poster so will provide the image and/or the physical poster.

It shows a crazy creature that looks like a skeleton having its head eaten by a tentacle creature.

SECOND POSTER TEXT
YOU are FOOD for THOUGHT
(logo)
MINUS Institute

BACK TO JENNA.

She's grasping, very tightly, a pamphlet. We can only read the phrase on the front.

INSERT PAMPHLET

NOTE: Gregory will design this pamphlet.

PAMPHLET
TAKE AWAY WHAT'S HOLDING YOU BACK

BACK TO JENNA

She's bouncing her leg, filled with nervous energy.

NURSE REBECCA enters the doorway with a clipboard. Looks at it and calls out.

NURSE REBECCA
Jenna?

YOU
are
FOOD
for
THOUGHT
MINUS
Institute

I CREATE MYSELF THROUGH WHAT I DO.
EXISTENCE PRECEDES ESSENCE
MINUS Institute

Jenna shoots up.

INT. NURSE REBECCA'S OFFICE - DAY

Jenna in another room, alone. Holding a clipboard with a completed form.

Nurse Rebecca enters and takes the clipboard from her, but trades it for another clipboard and form.

NURSE REBECCA
And this one.

Jenna looks the papers over and signs the release.

Nurse Rebecca takes it back, changes the paper, and returns it.

NURSE REBECCA (CONT'D)
And this one.

Jenna looks the new form over and jots on it and signs it. Returns it to Nurse Rebecca.

Nurse Rebecca hands her a plastic container.

NURSE REBECCA (CONT'D)
Fill this, please.

INT. BATHROOM - DAY

Jenna's just looking in the mirror.

Blankly.

Just staring.

Quiet. Not blinking.

Unnaturally sad.

Then startled into a blink by a sudden POUNDING ON THE DOOR.

Jenna's silent. Quiet. Staring.
So tired.
START

NOTE: Later, we'll hear the Dragon pounding with a hammer on a door after Jenna traps him temporarily. We should mirror the sound design of that later moment here.

INT. ANOTHER WAITING ROOM - DAY

There's a BUZZING TV SCREEN in the corner. No real picture on it. Just grainy non-images.

Still, Jenna's staring at it.

NOTE: During Jenna's run through the facility, later, from time to time we will see her on CCTV video, in grainy relief. This could begin HERE to establish the idea early. Such moments will NOT be noted in the script but should be noted by the second unit -- the editor will need options coverage of moments like this that can be used to build pace or tone but don't have obvious plot connections and so aren't always called out in the script.

Then Nurse Rebecca appears.

Nurse Rebecca hands Jenna another form.

The same blank look. Jenna's shoulders slump.

INT. NURSE REBECCA'S OFFICE - DAY

Jenna's silent. Quiet. Staring.

Starting to lose hope.

Sitting before a desk. An empty desk, an empty chair.

Looking tired. Dejected. Shoulders slumped.

She begins to blink, begins to drift.

Nodding off.

So tired.

NURSE REBECCA
(O.S.)
Wake up, Jenna.

Suddenly she's awake.

Sitting at the desk now is NURSE REBECCA.

It's like she appeared from thin air, but of course it's that Jenna fell asleep.

JENNA
Sorry.

NURSE REBECCA
Did you dream?

Jenna rubbing her eyes a bit.

JENNA
I don't think so, why?

NURSE REBECCA
(like it's obvious)
Dreams are dangerous.

Nurse Rebecca settles back and flips open a manilla file folder. Reviews her file.

NURSE REBECCA (CONT'D)
I'm sorry to tell you, Jenna, but based on your test results, the Minus Institute is denying your application for treatment.

Jenna looks about to cry but is holding it in.

JENNA
But it's getting worse.

NURSE REBECCA
I can see that. I *DO* want to help you Jenna. And I think I can.

Nurse Rebecca rises and walks to a nearby shelf.

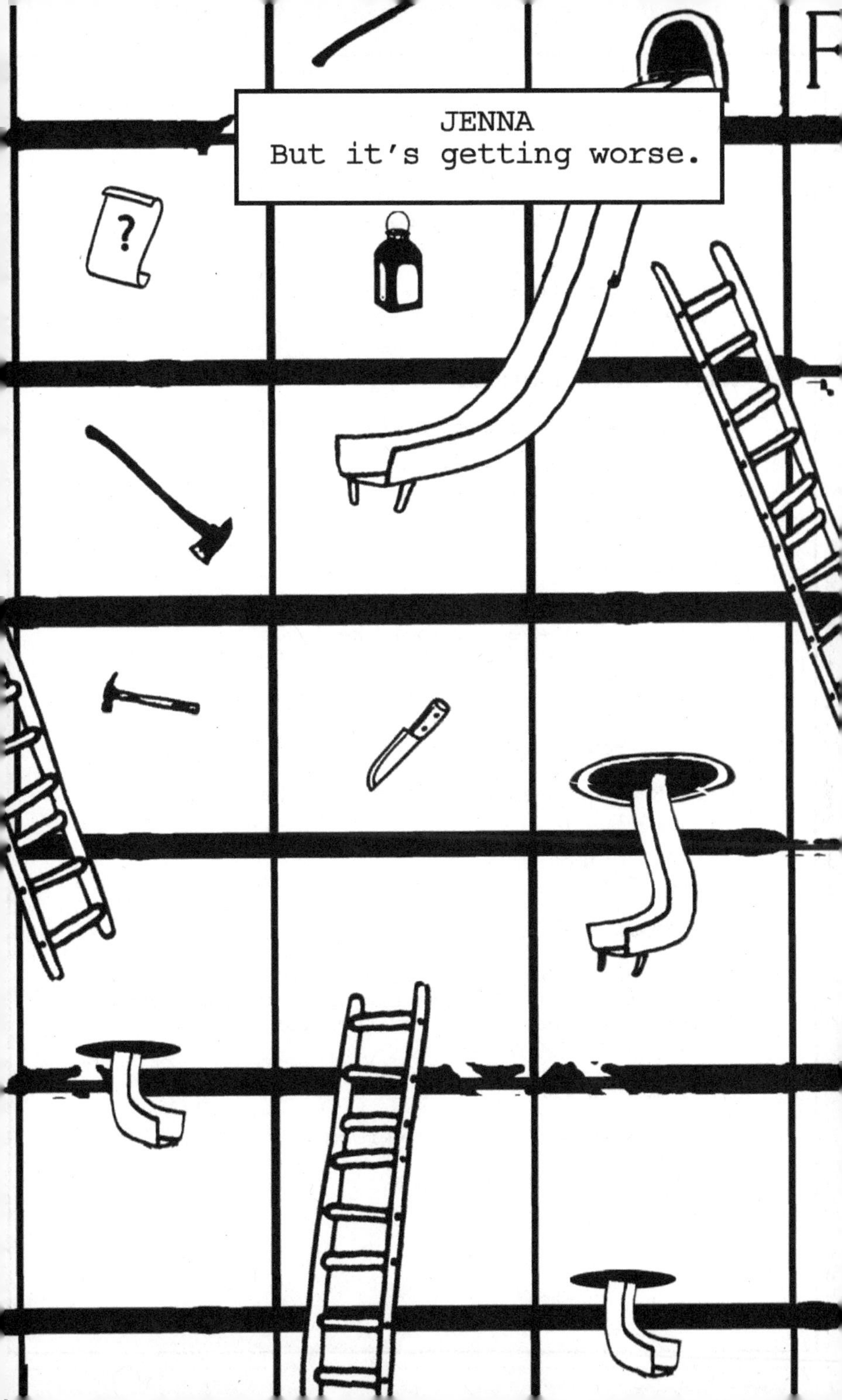
JENNA
But it’s getting worse.

NURSE REBECCA (CONT'D)
Although you are not right for the Institute's core treatment, we do have a sister program.

Nurse Rebecca takes down a pamphlet from the shelf and hands it to Jenna.

INSERT SECOND PAMPHLET

NOTE: Gregory will design this pamphlet.

PAMPHLET TEXT
THE STORYBOOK PROGRAM

BACK TO JENNA

NURSE REBECCA
I believe you would be a good fit, and would be willing to refer you.

JENNA
How do I--

Nurse Rebecca passes Jenna yet another clipboard.

JENNA (CONT'D)
Of course.

INT. JENNA'S ROOM - DAY

NOTE: Scenes are mostly listed as DAY rather than NIGHT but really the Director of Photography should determine a consistent look/feel for the lighting, whether day or night.

Jenna enters through an open door.

There's only a chair in the room.

On the chair is a STORYBOOK.

She looks around, like she's lost, confused.

She picks up the book. Sits down on the chair.

Opens it.

INSERT STORYBOOK

NOTE: Gregory will design this book.

The book is a picture book. In the book, we see a knight speaking to a princess.

The princess is holding up a key -- the key oversized, the images cartoonish.

KNIGHT SPEECH BUBBLE TEXT
What's a key without a lock?

BACK TO JENNA ON THE CHAIR

Suddenly startled by a voice, almost jumping out of her skin.

DR STORYBOOK
(O.S.)
Don't fall asleep.

INT. DOCTOR STORYBOOK'S OFFICE - DAY

A warmer room, a warmish man, DR STORYBOOK, walking around to sit at a desk.

Jenna's been sitting in a chair before the desk, now startled into attention.

DR STORYBOOK
I'm sure Nurse Rebecca warned you about dreams.

JENNA
Yes. But I don't quite understand.

TO CHANGE THE WORLD
YOU MUST FIRST
CHANGE YOURSELF.
If you can read this then you are different.
Don't sleepwalk through your life. Wake up.
Be changed.

MINUS
Institute

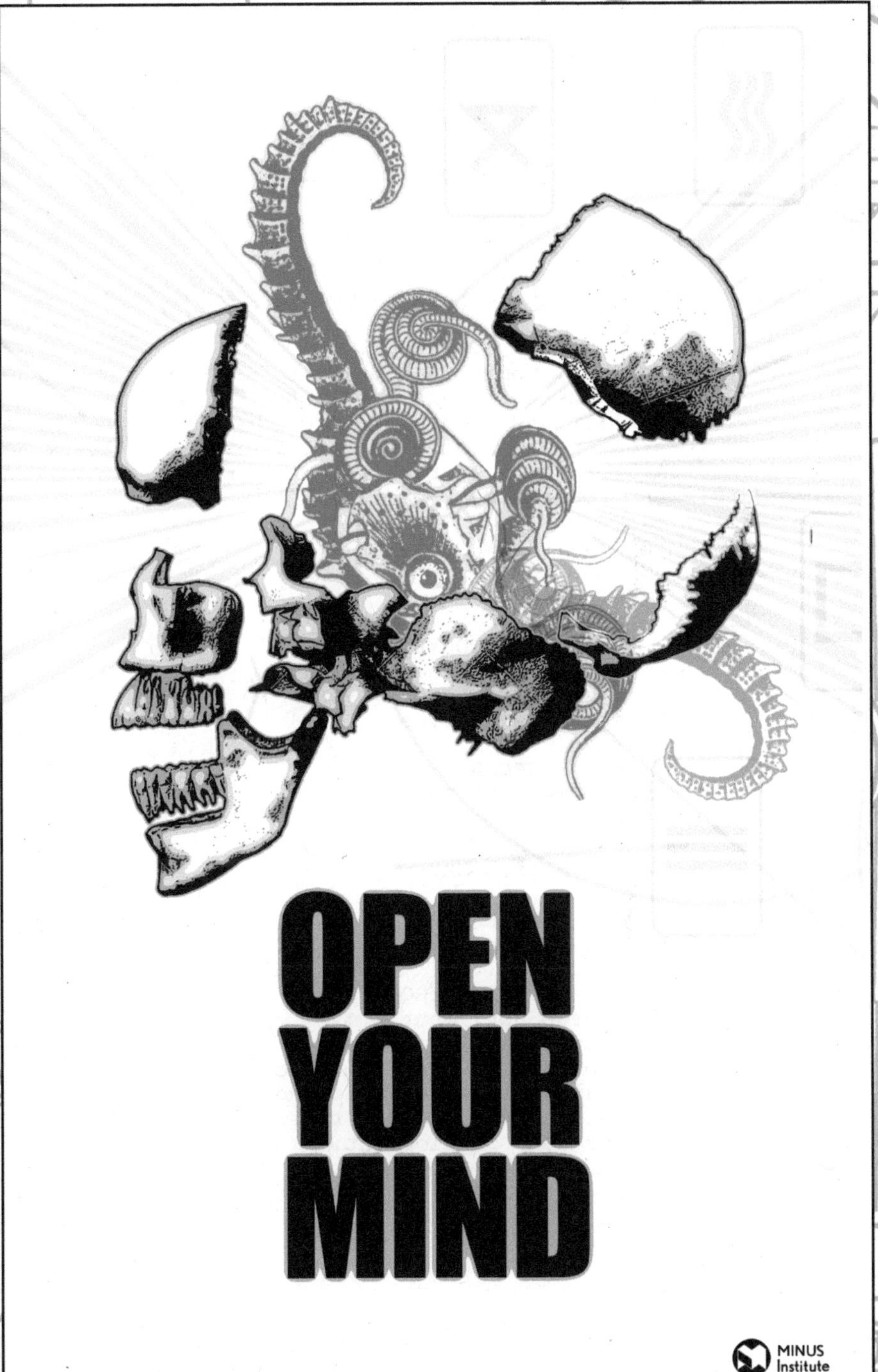

OPEN YOUR MIND

DR STORYBOOK
Part of your problem, Jenna, is that you're rejecting reality.

JENNA
Do you blame me?

Dr Storybook smiles, warmly.

DR STORYBOOK
In fact, your brain doesn't know the difference between reality and dreams. You could argue there's no difference. All of it is stories. The brain is programmed by stories.

JENNA
(not sure)
Sure.

DR STORYBOOK
And so part of the program, this program, is that you accept an archetype.

JENNA
Pardon me, uh, Doctor--

DR STORYBOOK
Doctor Storybook.

JENNA
That's your name?

DR STORYBOOK
Of course not. That's my archetype. As I was saying, this program -- The Storybook Program -- involves adopting an archetype as a useful framework for healthy development.

JENNA
I don't follow.

DR STORYBOOK
An archetype allows us to put a part of our personality 'over there' --

He gestures to the corner of the room.

Jenna follows the gesture but there's nothing there.

DR STORYBOOK (CONT'D)
(clearing his throat)
In a manner of speaking.
(going back to his explanation)
Then, we can look at this part of us, without judgment. So, I am "Dr. Storybook" and you can be "The Princess."

JENNA
I'm hardly a princess.

DR STORYBOOK
Again, all this is a conceptual framework. It lets us look at very serious things more easily.
(beat)
Your suicidal ideations. Imagine they are outside of you, but hunting you, like a Dragon in a fairytale.
(beat)
This Dragon has invaded your Castle. And a Dragon is scary, yes, it's monstrous, but it can be defeated.

JENNA
(almost crying, so confused)
I'm sorry. I don't know what you mean.

Dr Storybook stands. He walks around the desk.

Kneels down. To look Jenna right in the eye.

DR STORYBOOK
Yes you do, Jenna.

INT. JENNA'S ROOM - DAY

Suddenly, they're back in that empty room, with just the chair, Jenna seated there.

Dr Storybook kneeling to look in her face.

DR STORYBOOK
You must defeat the Dragon.

JENNA
Okay. Okay, but, isn't that what the Knight does? Prince Charming rescues the Princess.

DR STORYBOOK
Very good, Jenna. Very astute. See, I knew you would catch on quickly.
(he stands again)
Usually, yes, the Princess needs saving. And for you, perhaps, the Knight is the answer. If the Knight doesn't find you, you must find the Knight.

He lifts her hands into his, clasping them in front of her.

DR STORYBOOK (CONT'D)
My hope, of course, is that this Princess learns to save herself.

JENNA
So the Castle is me. But I'm inside the castle?

Dr Storybook lets her hands go and reaches behind himself.

Pulls a chair out of nowhere.

Sits down, across from her.

DR STORYBOOK
You're getting it so quickly!

JENNA
Where did--

DR STORYBOOK
(interrupting her)
You want to hurt yourself, because you believe you deserve it. That shame and that guilt and that confusion, these are the teeth of the dragon. You must cut away the Dragon's teeth--

Dr Storybook raises his hand, and holds a pill out to Jenna.

DR STORYBOOK (CONT'D)
--or the dragon will eat you up, my dear. And no one wants that.

Dr Storybook continues to hold the pill out to Jenna.

Jenna hesitates.

But she slowly, carefully, takes the pill from the smiling Dr Storybook.

WIDER, and now it's just Jenna, holding the pill.

Dr Storybook is gone. His chair gone too.

Jenna's confused. She rises.

Heads to the door, which is open.

BACK TO JENNA
Who notices she's holding the pill.
She resolves. She swallows it down.
START

Are you tired of feeling like a mere puppet in life? Break free from the shackles of doubt and indecision! Don't miss this opportunity to rewrite your destiny. Our cutting-edge brainwashing techniques will transform you into a confident, unstoppable force.

Thought Reform

Rapid Results: Witness the change within days!
Total Transformation: Say goodbye to old beliefs and embrace the new you.
Unleash Your Potential: Achieve success, wealth, and happiness effortlessly.

Send your intentions to the PSI Energy Commission

Pokes her head into the hallway.

INT. HALLWAY - NIGHT

WIDE, Jenna seems small in the long hallway.

It's empty. She's looking around.

We track CLOSER to her.

CLOSE. She's holding up the pill, but not paying attention to it, looking around.

REVERSE TO THE EMPTY HALLWAY

We see the empty hall from Jenna's POV.

NOTE: Please note that in places like this, directions are being given in the script that are rather detailed. These are just to suggest the intended pacing and mood and how the transitions could be accomplished in editing.

BACK TO JENNA

Who notices she's holding the pill.

She resolves. She swallows it down.

REVERSE TO THE EMPTY HALLWAY

TITLE CARD

CHAPTER II

IN THE CASTLE

INT. RUINED HALLWAY - DAY

The same shot, but the hallway is transformed. It was never spotless, but it was a "normal" hallway. Now, it's an absolute nightmare.

NOTE: The location includes the same basic hallway in two buildings, one more ruined than the other. The idea here is to add extra production value without extra expense by mirroring certain locations from the "cleaner/normal" building later with these ruined locations.

Disastrous, the walls peeling, floor covered in debris. Looking like a hundred years have passed, a hundred years of neglect and pain.

REVERSE and where Jenna had been standing in the hallway, now she's sitting on the chair again.

Wearing a large, BULKY PRINCESS DRESS, a stark contrast to the plain getup she had on before.

Wearing a strange, flat-white PRINCESS MASK.

CLOSER and we can see it's Jenna behind the mask.

We see she's also tied to the chair. Wrists and ankles bound.

Near her hand, a DAGGER has been stabbed into the arm of the chair.

Jenna slowly begins to rouse.

Looks around, in a haze.

Begins to realize her situation.

Jolts awake.

Almost falling backward from the jolt awake, panicking.

But catches herself before the chair falls over. Corrects herself.

Grounds the chair.

Grounds herself.

Begins shaking her head. Trying to dislodge the mask.

Violently shaking.

Finally, the mask dislodges.

CLOSE ON THE MASK

The Princess Mask crashes to the floor.

Jenna's free of that mask at least.

Jenna notices the knife.

Jenna goes to grab the knife but her wrist has been bound too tightly -- she can almost grab it by the handle, but is not quite able to reach it.

She wiggles her wrists. Tests the tightness of the bonds.

Tests her ankles too.

Notices the dress. Looks it over.

JENNA
(to herself)
Didn't think he meant Princess Peach.

Goes right back to wiggling her wrists, and trying to reach for the knife handle.

But she just can't reach it.

Then --

BEHIND HER

We see -- but she does NOT see -- THE DRAGON.

Another mask -- a DRAGON MASK -- on a hulking, dark form.

In the distance. A ways away from Jenna now.

Looming.

CLOSER to the Dragon, and we can see the mask up close. Angles and false teeth.

One hand of the Dragon holds A HAMMER, bobbing evilly as it walks closer and closer to Jenna.

The other hand of the Dragon holds AN AXE.

Then the Dragon begins to advance.

As it does, the axe drags. SCRAPING on the floor.

The SCRAPING SOUND catches Jenna's attention.

BACK TO JENNA

She's trying to turn and look behind her, where the Dragon is, where the sound comes from, but can't.

JENNA
(calling)
Dr Storybook?

Silence from the Dragon.

Just a slow advance.

But he doesn't need speed. Jenna is still tied to the chair.

JENNA (CONT'D)
(calling)
Nurse, uh--

She closes her eyes. Trying to remember.

JENNA (CONT'D)
(opening her eyes in a burst of remembering)
Rebecca!
(beat)
Rebecca, is that you?

Silence.

Scraping.

Jenna begins to freak out. Starts grabbing for the knife again, but again it's out of reach.

So she gives up trying to grab the handle.

CLOSE as Jenna clasps the knife's BLADE.

It hurts and she winces.

But she wiggles it.

Wiggles it.

Blood leaking through her fingers.

The Dragon advancing.

Jenna frees the knife.

It almost slips out of her hand!

But she gets her grip on it.

Slowly, carefully, Jenna maneuvers so she's grasping the blade with her bloody hand.

Wincing at the pain from the hand.

But able to saw the rope.

Sawing, sawing.

BEHIND JENNA

The Dragon is closer.

Closer.

Jenna cuts her one wrist free.

Quickly, quickly, the other wrist.

Her ankles.

The Dragon is CLOSER now.

CLOSER -- the Dragon rears back, begins the process of swinging the axe.

Jenna is free from the chair, rushing away.

Jenna looks over her shoulder, just as -- SMASH -- the axe bites into the chair, right where her head had been.

Jenna runs.

The Dragon delayed a moment while it frees the axe from the chair.

But Jenna also delayed. Tripping on the damn dress.

Jenna falls.

The Dragon has the axe free and is on her heels.

Jenna rises, runs, stumbles on the dress again.

Drops the knife this time.

The Dragon following.

Jenna crawls to the knife, recovers it.

Wincing as her hurt hand grasps it, moves it to the other hand.

Rising, but also cutting the bottom of the dress away.

The Dragon advancing. Swings the axe again. The axe bites into the floor, pinning the dress.

Pinning Jenna with the dress. But she turns, knife in hand.

Jenna stabs the Dragon in its leg.

The Dragon rears back, HOWLING INCOMPREHENSIBLY.

Jenna pulls the knife back when the Dragon rears away.

Using the knife, Jenna finishes cutting off the poofy bottom of the dress. Underneath she has warm, close-fitting layered clothes and sensible boots.

Still wearing the top part of the dress, over her shirt. She looks a mess.

Pulls away and runs just as the Dragon goes back on the attack. The Dragon swings the hammer into the space where Jenna was previously trapped by the dress.

Jenna rushes down the hallway.

The Dragon is also scraping his injured leg now. But never stopping. Coming closer.

Turns a corner.

NOTE: Remember! During Jenna's run through the facility, from time to time we see her on CCTV video, in grainy relief, here and there, to drive home the idea that she's being observed. This won't be noted in the script but should be noted by the second unit. Similarly, the second unit needs to just get shots of interesting on-set items and locations to give editing options.

INT. NEW HALLWAY - DAY

Around the corner, in a new hallway, Jenna rushes away from the Dragon.

Sees graffiti on the hallway wall:

GRAFFITI TEXT
NO GO

But someone's also scrawled a dripping/faded D on it, so that it can also read NO GOD.

NOTE: This graffiti is already present on location.

She rushes to the side, out of the hallway, through an open doorway.

INT. KITCHEN AREA - DAY

An abandoned, disused room that was clearly something like a facility kitchen, industrial sized, some remnants of industrial appliances here.

Breathing hard, Jenna looks everywhere. Flips over everything, looks in every cupboard.

She doesn't know what she's looking for. She's looking for anything.

Jenna slows a bit, thinking, taking the room in.

There's a MASSIVE DOOR with a BLUE DIAMOND marking it.

A small sign posted on the door. Almost comically, a warning sign.

INSERT DOOR WARNING SIGN

DOOR SIGN TEXT
This door MUST be kept closed

NOTE: This door and sign is already present on location.

BACK TO JENNA

Jenna grabs the handle, jostles it to try to open it, but of course it's locked, won't open.

She looks around for a weapon. Pushes debris around looking for something to grasp. Nothing is really that useful. Nothing better than the knife, for sure.

Jenna hears the SCRAPING down the hallway.

Rushes out of the room.

INT. DINING HALL - DAY

Across a large room is a massive bank of windows.

NOTE: Whenever we see windows in the background like this, bright sunlight is washing them out, so we can't really see outside of them.

Jenna makes her way toward the windows. She understands, right away, that this is a way out.

There are a few scattered chairs and tables in the dining hall -- overturned, broken, trash.

She grabs a chair as she gets closer to the window.

She throws the chair through the window without even looking out.

Then she does look out.

EXT. MINUS INSTITUTE - DAY

OUTSIDE, there's nothing, just a drop.

She's five stories up, at least.

The broken chair and glass are far below her.

Fuck.

She's not getting out this way.

INT. DINING HALL - DAY

Jenna looks out the dead-end window.

ON THE OTHER END OF THE ROOM, IN THE DOORWAY

The Dragon appears.

BACK TO JENNA

Jenna doesn't see the Dragon, but again, we can see it in the background.

She has her hands up to the window, looking out -- she's so close and yet so far.

The Dragon advances.

Jenna hears the scraping and turns to face it.

WIDE and we see them facing each other across the room.

Jenna holds up the knife.

CLOSER -- Jenna looking at the knife.

CLOSER on the Dragon -- Jenna looking at the axe, the hammer.

BACK TO THE KNIFE. It's better than nothing but obviously no match for the Dragon's weapons.

Jenna runs again.

TITLE CARD

CHAPTER III

THE KEY

INT. ANOTHER HALLWAY - DAY

Jenna's running, but slower, taking in her surroundings a bit more. Growing tired.

She grasps her hand. It's bloody still.

She grabs a strip from the princess dress top. Cuts it off.

Wraps her hand as best she can as she moves forward.

LOOKS INTO THE ROOMS SHE IS PASSING

They are mostly bedrooms, but without beds.

Trashed. Ruined.

Like the room she had been in before, where she had started, and was talking to Dr Storybook, before all this madness.

BACK TO JENNA

She slows. Stops.

Listens.

Hears nothing.

No scraping.

Begins to move again. Quieter.

She's getting in control of herself.

Realizing that she'll likely hear the Dragon before she sees it, that she has time to think, even if she doesn't have time to rest.

INT. RUINED RECEPTION AREA - DAY

Jenna stumbles out of the hall and into what clearly once used to be a reception area -- not the one she was in before, but a new place.

There's what seems to be a reception front desk. Empty, ruined.

NOTE: This reception desk/area is already present on location.

Jenna picks her way around the room. Looking for useful things. But it's all trash and broken objects.

She sees another hallway. Wider. Stranger.

Begins to move down it. Sees an odd room to her right. She enters it.

INT. VAULT ROOM - DAY

Inside this room is a massive Vault.

NOTE: This vault is already present on location.

Jenna stands before it. Stares at it.

JENNA
(quietly)
Dragons have treasure, right?
(beat)
Right, Jenna? Think.

She slowly approaches the Vault door. Carefully.

JENNA (CONT'D)
You're the Princess.

She reaches out to grasp the vault door's wheel lock.

IF YOU CAN SEE THE MAZE YOU ARE MEANT TO BE OUTSIDE OF IT.

You are an exception

THE WAY OUT IS WITHIN.

STAY STRONG

You cannot find the limits to

WHAT IS POSSIBLE

by asking permission.

MINUS
Institute

JENNA (CONT'D)
You must escape the Dragon.

She tests the door. The wheel of the vault begins to turn.

JENNA (CONT'D)
Gotta find the Knight.

Jenna finishes turning the wheel. Pulls the door open.

INT. VAULT - DAY

Behind the door --

Inside the vault --

A DEAD PRINCESS HANGS.

She's a corpse. Dead a while.

She's wearing the same dress, the one Jenna cut away.

She's wearing the mask still, the one Jenna threw on the ground.

She's tied by ropes to the ceiling. There's a similar knife stabbed near her hands.

Jenna reaches up, pulls out the knife. Now she has two.

Holding two knives hurts though. Her hand still hurts. She puts the new knife down.

She cuts another strip from her dress like she did to bandage her hand.

She ties the new strip into a makeshift belt and straps the knives to herself this way. Now she can free her hands to inspect the vault.

The vault is cramped. Wooden shelves surround the corpse of the previous princess.

These shelves are lined with rotting files.

NOTE: These rotting/old files are already present on location.

Jenna begins to dig through them.

Looking for clues.

Sifting through the rotting files. One catches her eye. It seems newer than the others.

She pulls it out. Opens the file.

INSERT THE FILE

We can see it's a transcript of Jenna talking to Dr Storybook. Her interview from before. Her intake.

Nothing new here. But creepy as shit.

BACK TO JENNA

She flips through. Nothing she doesn't know. Literally her own words staring back at her.

INSERT THE HANGING CORPSE

Jenna studies it, takes a second look.

CLOSE ON THE ARM of the previous princess.

Her arm is ripped open. Bloody.

Jenna looks more closely.

INSERT KEY TATTOO

There's a KEY TATTOO on the arm, just above where it's been cut open.

BACK TO JENNA

Jenna looks down at her own arm.

She hikes up her sleeve.

She sees the SAME KEY TATTOO ... and, underneath it, a scar.

Jenna backs away, as if struck.

INT. VAULT ROOM - DAY

Backing away from the vault. From the dead, previous princess with the cut-open arm.

Jenna is stunned. Looking at her arm.

But then comes to her senses.

She is sick of looking at the corpse and closes the door again.

She takes out one of the knives.

She holds the tip up to her arm, near the scar, near the Key Tattoo.

Closes her eyes like she's going to push -- then stops.

Opens her eyes.

JENNA
(whispering)
What's a key without a lock?
(beat)
Fuck.

Backs the knife away.

TITLE CARD

The Princess and the Dragon

THE LOCK

INT. FACILITY - DAY

NOTE: When location is vague, like "Facility," there is not a precise room at the location that is being thought about and different rooms could be used to give a false sense of massive scale.

Jenna wanders through the facility, through large rooms with no clear purpose.

She sees a light in a distant storeroom and approaches it.

INT. STOREROOM - DAY

Inside the storeroom, we see a massive freezer. Lid up, open.

To the left of the freezer is a cold room door, with a big piece of wood holding it shut.

JENNA

Nope.

She leaves the room.

NOTE: This freezer and the cold room beside it are already present on location.

NOTE: This scene sets up the later scene so is essential despite there being little plot in this moment.

INT. ANOTHER HALLWAY - DAY

Jenna exploring.

Making her way through the facility.

She spies a stairwell in the distance.

INT. STAIRWELL - DAY

Hopeful, Jenna rushes over.

Jenna runs

DOWN THE STAIRS

but they're blocked.

A massive door in the way.

She bangs on it in frustration.

Gives up. Tries going

UP THE STAIRS TO THE NEXT FLOOR

But further up, there's just another massive door.

She's trapped in this floor.

Sighing, dejected.

Moves back down the stairs.

NOTE: The intention here is to suggest that all areas we see exist on one floor, and thus the entire facility is impossibly massive and confusingly laid out -- the vibe here being that this is like a labyrinth with a minotaur in it.

BACK ON THE MAIN FLOOR

we see the Dragon is hidden in a shadowed area beside the stairs.

NOTE: This area is already present on location.

Jenna doesn't see the Dragon but we do.

She's off her guard, dejected.

As she nears the Dragon, he springs forward, flailing his weapons.

Jenna's just fast enough to avoid the reach of the weapons by ducking into him -- closer, inside of his swing -- but now he's on top of her.

They smash down to the floor.

One of the knives falls loose and tumbles down the stairwell to the floor below.

The Dragon flailing to hurt her with the hammer. She keeps tucked inside of its reach while she scrambles out the other knife.

But as she's trying to get it out the Dragon's body mashes hers down, and her injured hand is hurt again.

She shrieks in pain as the Dragon flails at her.

She frees the knife and slashes at him.

The Dragon rears back -- flailing again -- but as it does it knocks her remaining knife away with the hammer.

She backs off, rising, putting some distance between them.

The Dragon also rises.

The knife is behind the Dragon now. Jenna's defenceless.

The Dragon is injured. CLOSE ON where she slashed it.

The sleeve of the Dragon's ragged outfit is slashed open now and we can see more skin.

INSERT

The Dragon has the same Key Tattoo -- we can see this, and Jenna can see it too, now that the sleeve has been cut away somewhat.

BACK TO JENNA

She begins to speak to the Dragon.

Clearly. Calmly. Reasoning with it.

JENNA
Okay. So you're trapped here too. Like me.

She gestures back and forth between them.

JENNA (CONT'D)
We're the same, yeah? We can work together.

The Dragon ROARS -- although it's really something between a wet gurgle and a muffled scream. Nothing articulate.

But she keeps trying to reason with it. They're circling each other a little.

JENNA (CONT'D)
We have keys, yeah. We can get out. We just need the lock.

The Dragon ROARS again.

JENNA (CONT'D)
(as if she understood)
Whose key, though, sure, I get it.

The Dragon BANGS its hammer into the wall.

JENNA (CONT'D)
We can worry about that later.

She's circled closer to the knife and lunges for it.

But the Dragon SLAMS its axe in front of her, blocking her path to the knife.

Jenna backs up.

JENNA (CONT'D)
You've got two weapons. I've got none.

The Dragon roars.

JENNA (CONT'D)
Let me have the knife and I'll trust you.

The Dragon cocks its head. Is it listening? Does it understand?

Jenna begins to move, slowly, in the direction of the knife.

She has to come closer to the Dragon to do so.

She does so. Moving slowly.

JENNA (CONT'D)
You don't have to be the Dragon.

Jenna moves closer. Cautious.

JENNA (CONT'D)
You can be the Knight.

The Dragon seems almost convinced. It seems calmer.

She moves closer.

But she's so close now. Too close.

Too tempting.

The Dragon realizes it could have her.

And it swings -- Jenna grabs the hammer-arm in mid-swing.

Tries to take the hammer -- but gets slammed in the wall.

The axe comes up -- misses her -- bites the wall.

Now the Dragon has both weapons stuck in the wall.

Jenna lunges under the weapons and begins to rush off -- but then pauses. She looks back.

For some reason, the Dragon is not letting go of the axe or the hammer, both of which have gone into the drywall and gotten stuck there.

It's wriggling like a bug.

Jenna takes advantage of this moment to recover the knife.

Then she rushes away just as the Dragon gets one of the weapons loose and is pulling at the other.

INT. ANOTHER HALLWAY - DAY

Jenna's running.

Running.

Putting more distance between her and the Dragon.

INT. FURNACE ROOM - DAY

Jenna finds a furnace room --

-- is about to back out but sees a HOLE on the other side.

NOTE: This furnace room and the hole in its wall are already present at the location.

She checks behind her, listening for the Dragon.

Hears nothing.

She moves further into the room.

Crosses to explore the HOLE.

INT. HOLE - DAY

There's a hole smashed into the cement wall.

NOTE: This hole in the concrete wall is already present at the location.

She pushes her body in -- but there's no exit here.

She backs out.

But then as she's about leave, notices something.

Reaches into the hole.

Pulls out a STORYBOOK.

INT. FURNACE ROOM - DAY

It's the storybook she was looking at earlier, before entering the program.

She takes a closer look at it now.

INSERT STORYBOOK COVER

TITLE TEXT
The Princess and the Dragon

BACK TO JENNA

Jenna looks at the book, remembering.

JENNA
What's a key without a lock?

Jenna flips open the book to find that page.

INSERT PAGE WITH THE KNIGHT

Again, the page she had stopped on earlier.

JENNA TURNS THE PAGE

And again, the Knight talking to the Princess in the book.

KNIGHT DIALOGUE BUBBLE TEXT
The Treasure's behind the Blue Door!

Jenna looks up from the book.

FLASHING BACK

The door she wasn't able to open earlier, with the blue diamond.

BACK TO JENNA

She hadn't been looking for a locked door then, and overlooked it later.

Jenna closes the book. Eyes darting about.

Thinking.

TITLE CARD

CHAPTER V

THE KNIGHT

INT. LARGE ROOMS FILLED WITH DEBRIS - DAY

Jenna walks through, tossing debris. Looking for another weapon.

Under some trash, she finds a large WOODEN PADDLE -- the kind a schoolmaster would use to spank a child.

NOTE: This paddle is already present at the location.

Jenna gives the paddle a few test swings.

JENNA
This'll do.

She walks over to a metal table in the corner.

Jenna begins to whack the metal table with the paddle. Making a METAL BANGING SOUND.

Shouting into the facility.

JENNA (CONT'D)
Damsel in distress!

She stops pounding. Listens.

Nothing.

Begins pounding on the metal table again.

JENNA (CONT'D)
Dinner is served!

Stops. Listens.

Hears the SCRAPING again.

Turns in its direction.

ON THE OTHER END OF THE ROOM

The Dragon is stumbling after her.

BACK TO JENNA

She goes to put her second hand on the paddle, holding it two-handed. But winces. The pain in her hand is getting worse.

She's back to one-handing the paddle, but it's awkward.

She looks like she might take a swing at the advancing Dragon, but instead she runs.

The Dragon lopes after her.

INT. FACILITY - DAY

Through the facility, filled with junk. Jenna pushes things over as she goes.

The Dragon follows.

Jenna runs into a storeroom.

The Dragon keeps after her, his pace steady.

INT. STOREROOM - DAY

The Dragon follows Jenna into the storeroom.

Jenna isn't in sight.

It's the same storeroom as before, with the massive freezer. Lid up, open.

To the left of the freezer is the same cold room door -- but the big piece of wood holding it shut is off to the side and the door is slightly ajar.

The Dragon makes its way toward the cold room door.

The Dragon awkwardly uses its hammer to hook where the door is ajar and pull it open.

But Jenna's not inside.

Instead, Jenna rushes out from behind the freezer.

She's got the big paddle. She brings it down on the back of the Dragon's head.

Knocking him forward -- also pushing, kicking him.

The Dragon staggers into the cold room.

Jenna pushes the door shut. Blocks it up with the wood.

The Dragon begins to POUND on the door with its hammer, a LET-ME-OUT pound.

INT. FACILITY - DAY

Jenna gets out of the storeroom.

The same LET-ME-OUT POUND coming from the cold room inside the storeroom.

Jenna closes the storeroom door. Now there are two doors between her and the Dragon.

But then the sound changes. Now the Dragon is using the axe, it's a CHOPPING OUT SOUND.

Jenna jams this second door shut with the paddle.

She rushes away.

INT. LARGE ROOMS FILLED WITH DEBRIS - DAY

Jenna rushing through the rooms, backtracking.

The CHOPPING OUT SOUND seems louder, even though it's farther away.

Jenna doesn't have time to rest.

INT. KITCHEN - DAY

Finally, she's back in the kitchen area.

Again, we see the locked door with the blue diamond on it.

Jenna stands before the door.

She rolls her sleeve up.

She lifts up her arm.

She readies her knife above the key tattoo.

YOU WILL LEARN TO RECOGNIZE A BAD IDEA

She's about to cut into her arm for the key...

... but she's not doing it.

In the distance, faint now, the CHOPPING OUT SOUND.

She looks away from her arm. Back to where the sound's coming from.

INT. FACILITY - DAY

Outside the storeroom door now.

The CHOPPING LOUD.

AT THE WALL

CHOP.

CHOP.

And then -- CHOP through the wall.

Another CHOP -- the hole bigger.

BACK TO JENNA

Jenna's standing there.

Watching.

Waiting.

Not running any more.

She's made this decision.

She has a plan.

THROUGH THE WALL

The axe bursts entirely through.

We see the Dragon's mask beginning to push through.

BACK TO JENNA

She slams the axe-arm against the edge of the hole.

She stabs the knife down into the Dragon's arm.

Jenna begins to pull the axe away.

JENNA
Give me that you fu--

Now that she's close, she gets a closer look.

INSERT THE DRAGON'S HAND

There's a metal wire that runs through a hole in the axe-handle--

-- and the metal wire also runs THROUGH the Dragon's hand.

These weapons are literally hooked into the Dragon's body with a primitive, painful-looking piercing.

They go right through the palms, there is flesh and bone and blood in the way of getting these weapons out.

If the Dragon even loosens his grip, they pull at his flesh, this is a mastermind of pain and torment kind of design.

She's not getting them off.

Or is she?

JENNA
You poor man.

Jenna just fucking goes to town and rips the hammer right out of his flesh along with the piercing!

The Dragon ROARS!!!

Then she turns right around and smashes the fucking guy with the hammer.

She knocks him out. He slumps.

Appearing dead.

JENNA (CONT'D)
You should have joined me.

She gets her knife ready to push into his arm, where the key tattoo is.

INT. KITCHEN - DAY

Jenna's got a bloody key in her bloody hand.

Standing before the blue-diamond door.

She unlocks it.

She pulls the door open.

INSIDE THE DOOR

The word HELP is scrawled on the inside.

NOTE: This graffiti is already present at the location.

Jenna steps past this warning, into the room.

INT. BLUE DOOR ROOM - DAY

It's not the exit she expects, that we expect.

She's frustrated. In the room. Looking around.

Inside the room, there's a weird container that is made of metal and looks like some sort of combination between a tanker and a vault.

NOTE: This container is already present at the location.

It has a turning wheel lock with metal spindles.

Jenna looks at the container/vault thing.

She grabs the wheel/lock.

Wincing at the pain that's still in her bloody hand.

She turns the wheel.

INSERT THE SPINDLES TURNING WITH THE WHEEL

Jenna unlocks the container.

She looks inside.

Reaches inside.

Pulls out a REVOLVER.

INSERT THE REVOLVER

In her hand, on the gun, we see a KNIGHT SYMBOL etched on the handle.

Jenna unloads the gun.

There's only ONE BULLET.

She looks at the bullet.

JENNA
(hopelessly)
The Knight saves the Princess.

She reloads the gun.

Then we hear the SCRAPING of the Dragon, behind her.

Jenna turns.

IN THE DOORWAY, THE DRAGON STANDS

Bloody. Barely alive.

But still following her.

Jenna raises the loaded gun.

It's now under her chin, pointing up.

BUT...

... Jenna straightens her arm and points the gun at the Dragon.

CRASH TO BLACK

As we crash to black, we hear the SOUND OF THE GUN FIRING.

TITLE CARD

CHAPTER VI

THE DRAGON

INT. BLUE DOOR ROOM - DAY

Moments later.

The Dragon is on the ground.

Jenna drops her arm.

She drops the now-useless gun.

Jenna steps toward the Dragon. Kneels down near him.

Lifts up his head.

Takes off his mask.

INSERT THE DRAGON'S FACE

His mouth is STITCHED SHUT.

JENNA
I wonder what you were trying to say.

She drops the Dragon's face back down.

She stands.

Jenna steps over the body of the Dragon and leaves the room.

INT. KITCHEN - DAY

Jenna exits -- but immediately is set upon by a GROUP OF MEN -- they seem like they come out of nowhere.

JENNA
(spiteful)
So now what?

They're in white coats, like lab coats almost -- she kicks, punches with her good hand -- they come at her anyway.

She breaks free of them, injures one. He backs off.

JENNA (CONT'D)
What now?

But they are back on her.

She struggles but there are too many.

JENNA (CONT'D)
Get off!

Nurse Rebecca appears in the melee -- she's got a needle and she plunges it into the struggling and shouting Jenna.

INT. JENNA'S ROOM - DAY

Hauled back into her room, she's on the chair again.

Tied to it again.

Wakened by pain -- as they wire/pierce weapons to her hand, just like they did to the Dragon before her -- in this case, though it's the knife she was using, as well as the hammer she took from the last Dragon.

Jenna SHRIEKS in pain as the men keep working, wiring the weapons to her hands.

Another man readies a needle and thread.

DR STORYBOOK steps into the room.

DR STORYBOOK
You're cured! Look at you. I've never seen such progress, such a will to live.

JENNA
I won! I saved MYSELF!

DR STORYBOOK
(like he didn't hear her)
And now you'll help others.

JENNA
It's over!

DR STORYBOOK
True stories are cycles. And cycles continue. A true story never ends.

JENNA
You think I won't end this? I'll tell YOU a goddamn story!

Dr Storybook looks uncertain. Unsure.

46.

JENNA (CONT'D)
I don't stop. I don't hesitate. I'm not the princess, who needs saving. I'm not the knight, who'll save you.

One of the men readies the mask.

She spits on the mask. The man holding it is taken aback. He's never seen this.

JENNA (CONT'D)
And I'm not the dragon.

Shouting. Defiant. Furious.

JENNA (CONT'D)
I'm the fire inside!

CRASH TO BLACK

CRASH TO BLACK

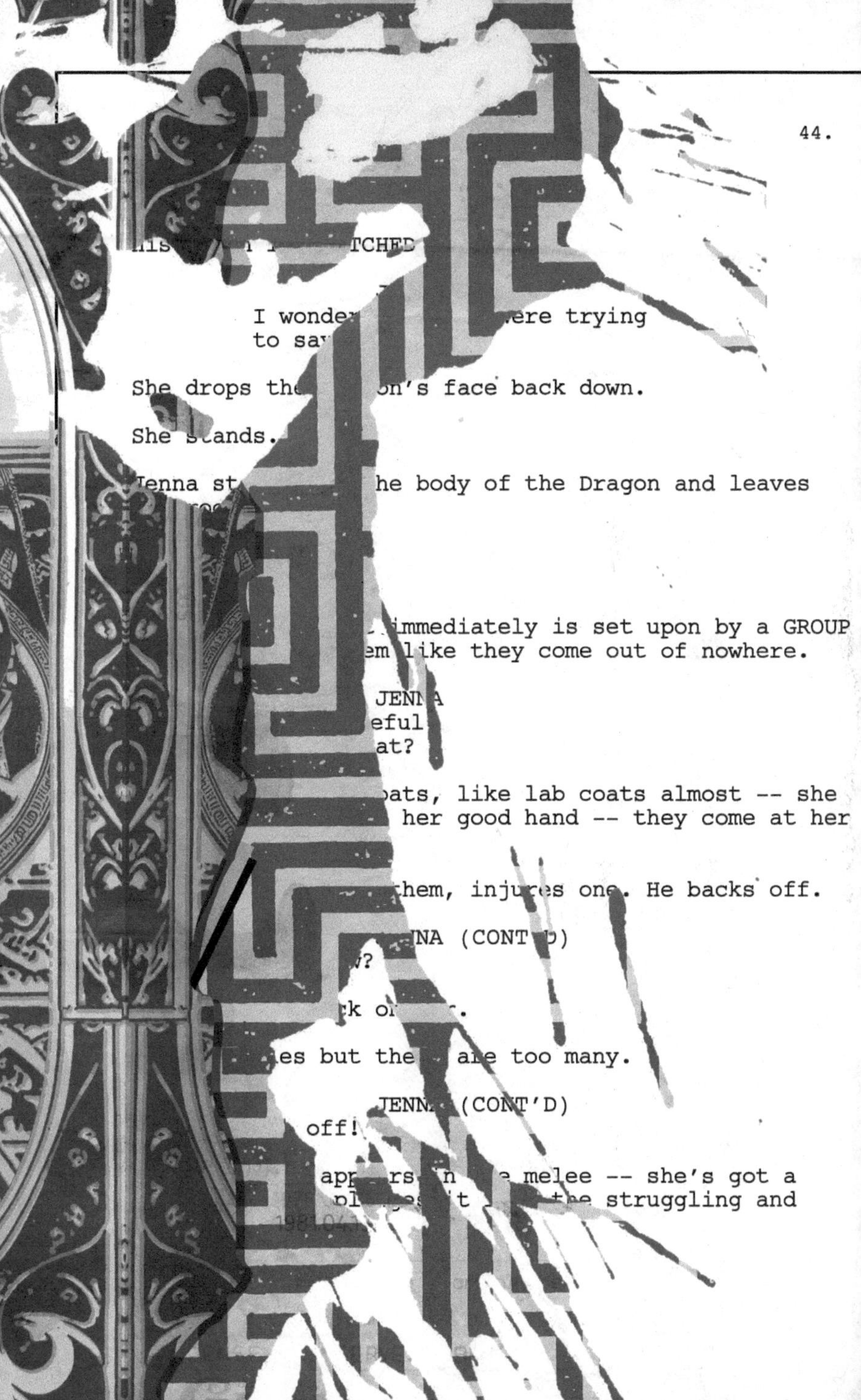

HIS ... TCHED

I wonde... ere trying
to sa...

She drops the ... on's face back down.

She stands.

Jenna st... he body of the Dragon and leaves

... immediately is set upon by a GROUP
... em like they come out of nowhere.

JENNA
... eful
... at?

... oats, like lab coats almost -- she
... her good hand -- they come at her

... them, injures one. He backs off.

...NA (CONT'D)
...?

...k o...

...es but the... are too many.

JENNA (CONT'D)
... off!

... appears in ... melee -- she's got a
... plunges it ... the struggling and

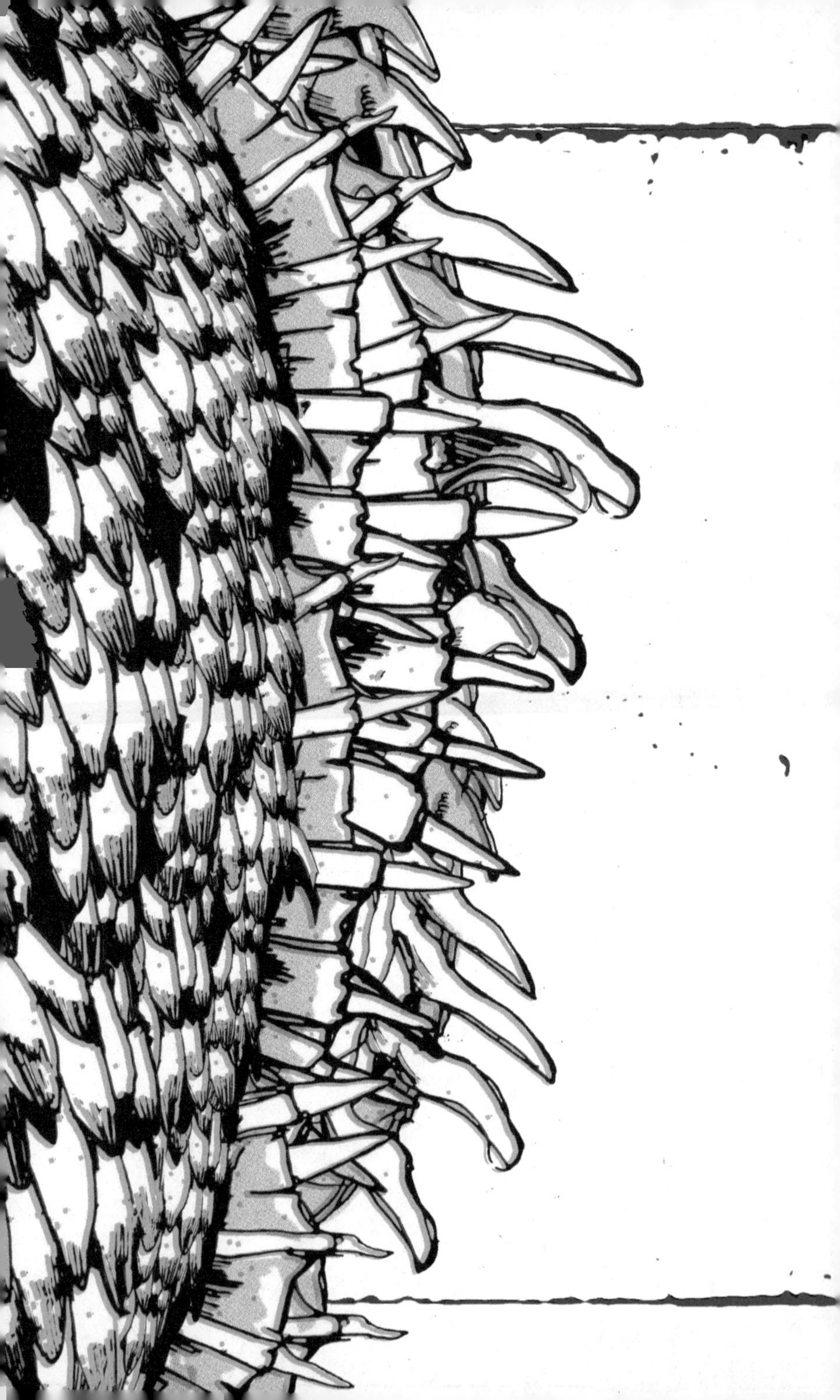

START

“The entrance to the facility is safe and ordered. Suggesting control and reason.”

“Clean and bright.”

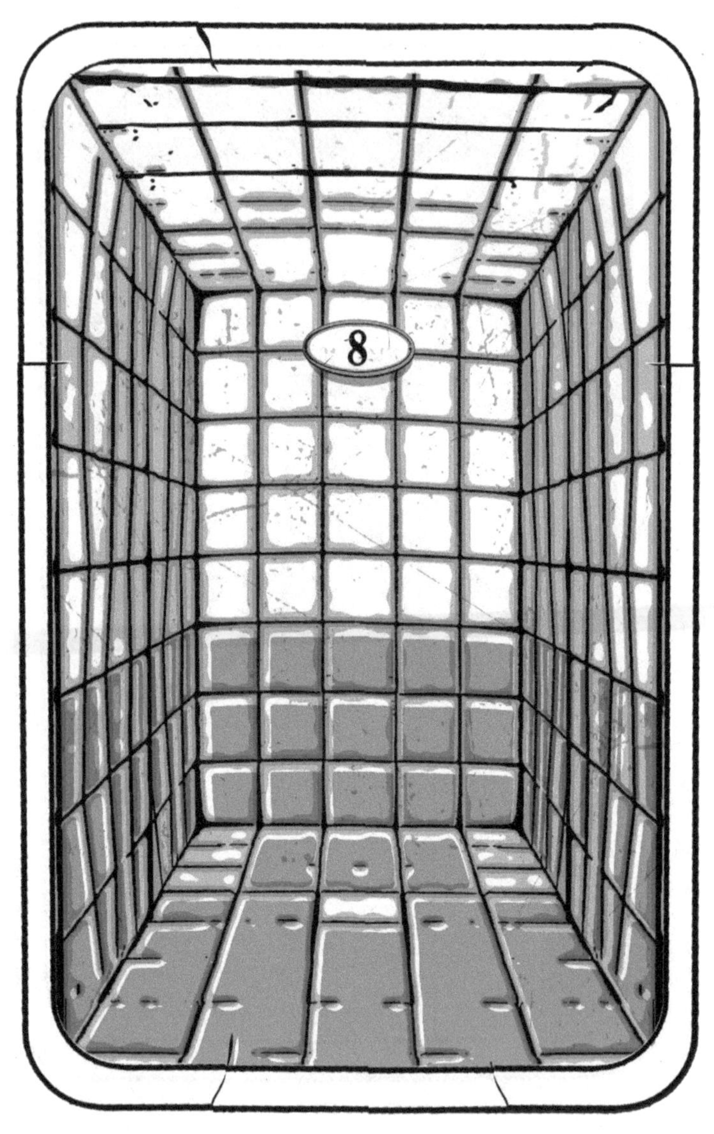

“There is a kind of comfort so effective that it is not altogether welcoming. Enclosure provokes wandering.”

“It is the invitation to descend from safe spaces that is the most necessary part of the story.”

“Then a further invitation.”

“It begins to be a very minor thing to connect the descent of the body with the ascent of the mind. The conditioned emotional response to danger is thus converted to a curiosity to explore the edges of one’s own safety.”

“Which can eventually be encouraged to include the edges of one’s own body.”

“They return with the ability to reorder both themselves and the world around them. A successful self-actualization.”

ESCAPE FROM THE FAIRY TALE

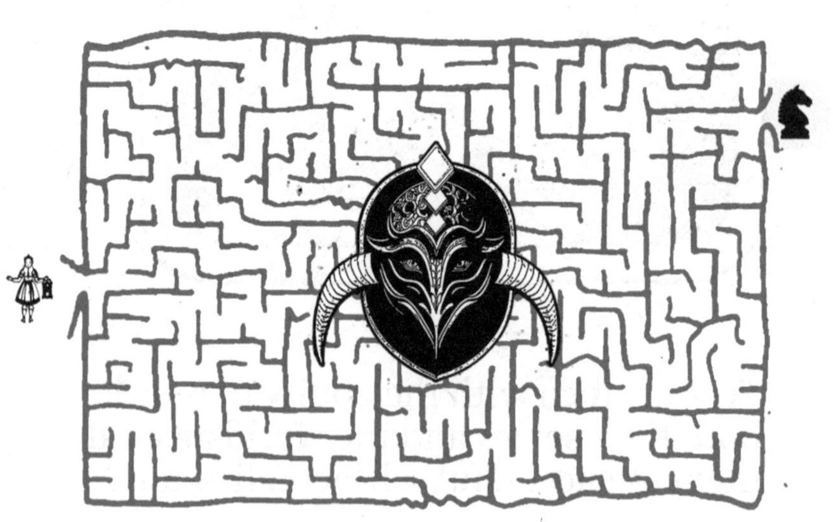

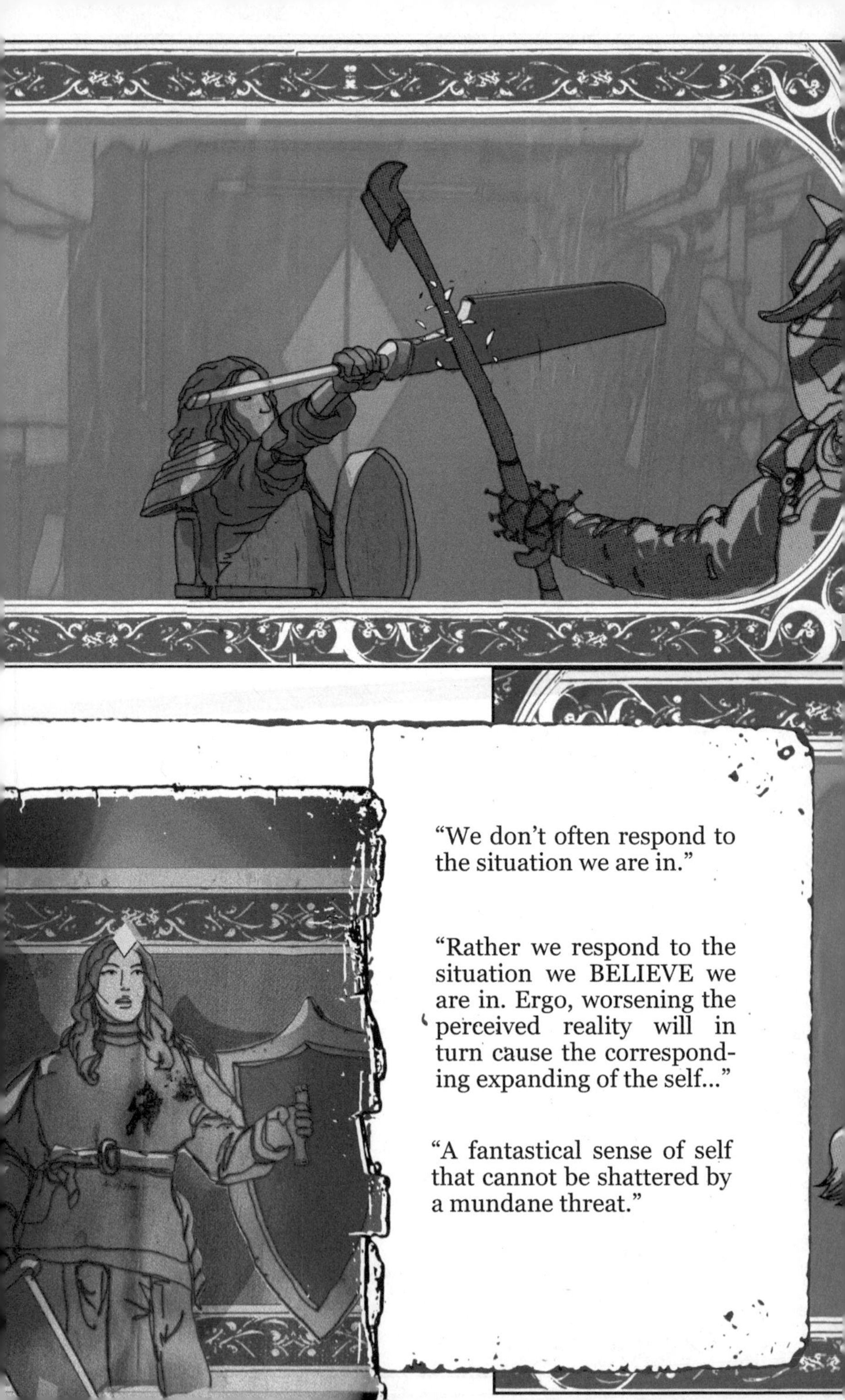
"We don't often respond to the situation we are in."
"Rather we respond to the situation we BELIEVE we are in. Ergo, worsening the perceived reality will in turn cause the corresponding expanding of the self..."
"A fantastical sense of self that cannot be shattered by a mundane threat."

"It is vital that the truth of the situation only be the basic form that the experience is built upon."

"A portion of all confidence is delusion guided by imagination. One 'hopes they can before they know they can'."

"Confidence is a key to success but it is easily shattered."

"A mythical sense of self requires
a legendary reality."

"If you can..."

ESCAPE FROM THE FAIRY TALE

"Imagine what else you could accomplish?"